THE ADVENTURES OF THE GRAND VIZIER IZNOGOUD
BY GOSCINNY & TABARY

THE
GRAND VIZIER
IZNOGOUD

SCRIPT: GOSCINNY   **DRAWING: TABARY**

CINEBOOK

Original title: Le grand Vizir Iznogoud

Original edition: © Dargaud Editeur Paris, 1966, by Goscinny & Tabary
www.dargaud.com
All rights reserved

English translation: © 2012 Cinebook Ltd

Translator: Jerome Saincantin
Lettering and text layout: Imadjinn sarl
Printed in Spain by Just Colour Graphic

This edition published in Great Britain in 2012 by
Cinebook Ltd
56 Beech Avenue,
Canterbury, Kent
CT4 7TA
www.cinebook.com

A CIP catalogue record for this book
is available from the British Library

978-1-84918-131-0

9th CINEBOOK
The 9th Art Publisher

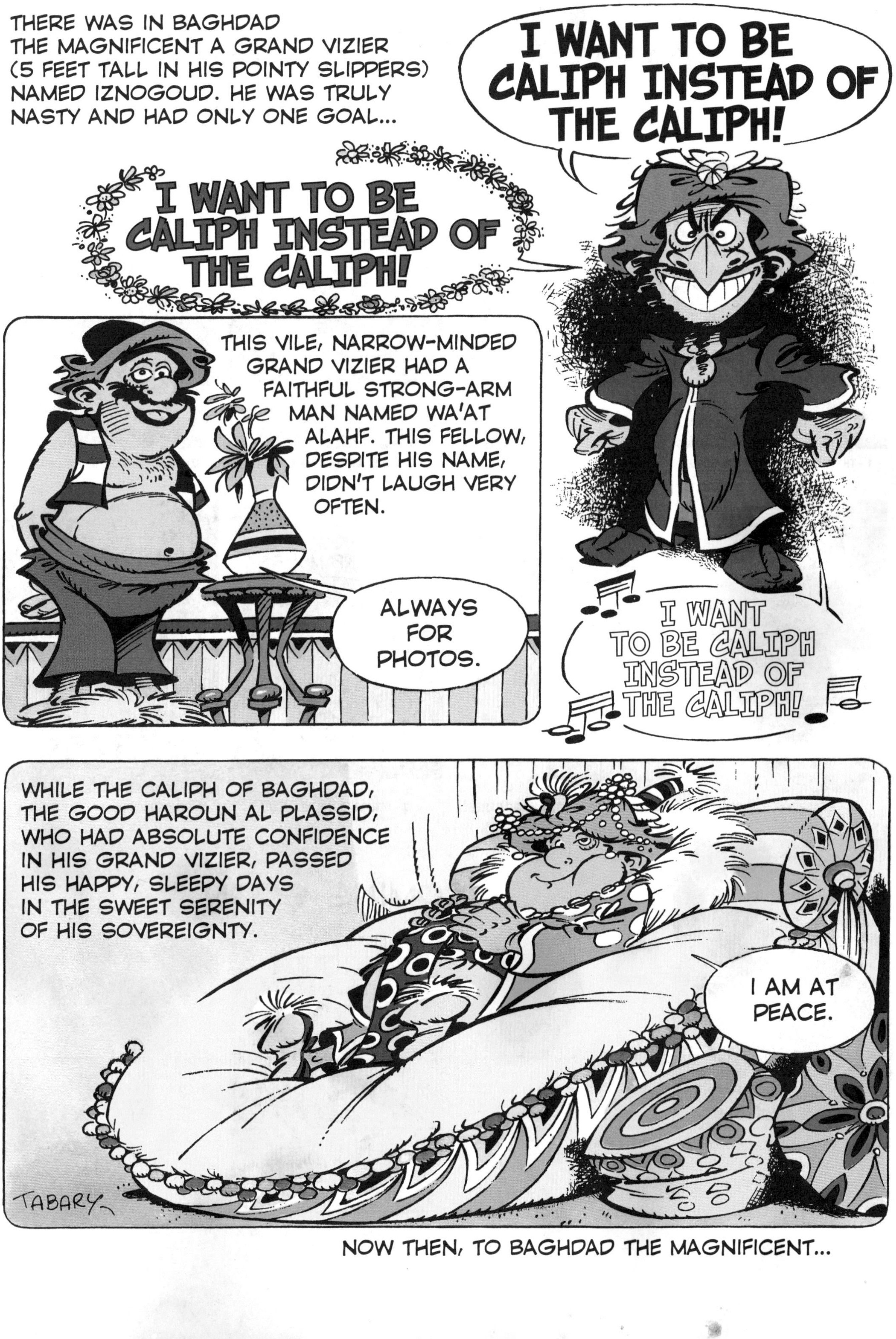
THERE WAS IN BAGHDAD THE MAGNIFICENT A GRAND VIZIER (5 FEET TALL IN HIS POINTY SLIPPERS) NAMED IZNOGOUD. HE WAS TRULY NASTY AND HAD ONLY ONE GOAL...
I WANT TO BE CALIPH INSTEAD OF THE CALIPH!
I WANT TO BE CALIPH INSTEAD OF THE CALIPH!
THIS VILE, NARROW-MINDED GRAND VIZIER HAD A FAITHFUL STRONG-ARM MAN NAMED WA'AT ALAHF. THIS FELLOW, DESPITE HIS NAME, DIDN'T LAUGH VERY OFTEN.
ALWAYS FOR PHOTOS.
I WANT TO BE CALIPH INSTEAD OF THE CALIPH!
WHILE THE CALIPH OF BAGHDAD, THE GOOD HAROUN AL PLASSID, WHO HAD ABSOLUTE CONFIDENCE IN HIS GRAND VIZIER, PASSED HIS HAPPY, SLEEPY DAYS IN THE SWEET SERENITY OF HIS SOVEREIGNTY.
I AM AT PEACE.
TABARY
NOW THEN, TO BAGHDAD THE MAGNIFICENT...

IZNOGOUD

GOSCINNY - TABARY
THE WICKED WILES OF
IZNOGOUD

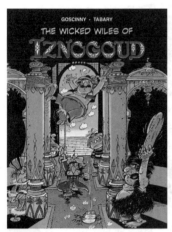

1 - THE WICKED WILES OF IZNOGOUD

GOSCINNY - TABARY
IZNOGOUD
THE CALIPH'S VACATION

2 - THE CALIPH'S VACATION

GOSCINNY - TABARY
IZNOGOUD
AND THE DAY OF MISRULE

3 - IZNOGOUD AND THE DAY OF MISRULE

GOSCINNY - TABARY
IZNOGOUD
AND THE MAGIC COMPUTER

4 - IZNOGOUD AND THE MAGIC COMPUTER

GOSCINNY - TABARY
A CARROT FOR
IZNOGOUD

5 - A CARROT FOR IZNOGOUD

GOSCINNY - TABARY
IZNOGOUD
AND THE MAGIC CARPET

6 - IZNOGOUD AND THE MAGIC CARPET

GOSCINNY - TABARY
IZNOGOUD
THE INFAMOUS

7 - IZNOGOUD THE INFAMOUS

GOSCINNY - TABARY
IZNOGOUD
ROCKETS TO STARDOM

8 - IZNOGOUD ROCKETS TO STARDOM

GOSCINNY - TABARY
THE GRAND VIZIER
IZNOGOUD

9 - THE GRAND VIZIER IZNOGOUD

COMING SOON

GOSCINNY - TABARY
IZNOGOUD
THE RELENTLESS

10 - IZNOGOUD THE RELENTLESS

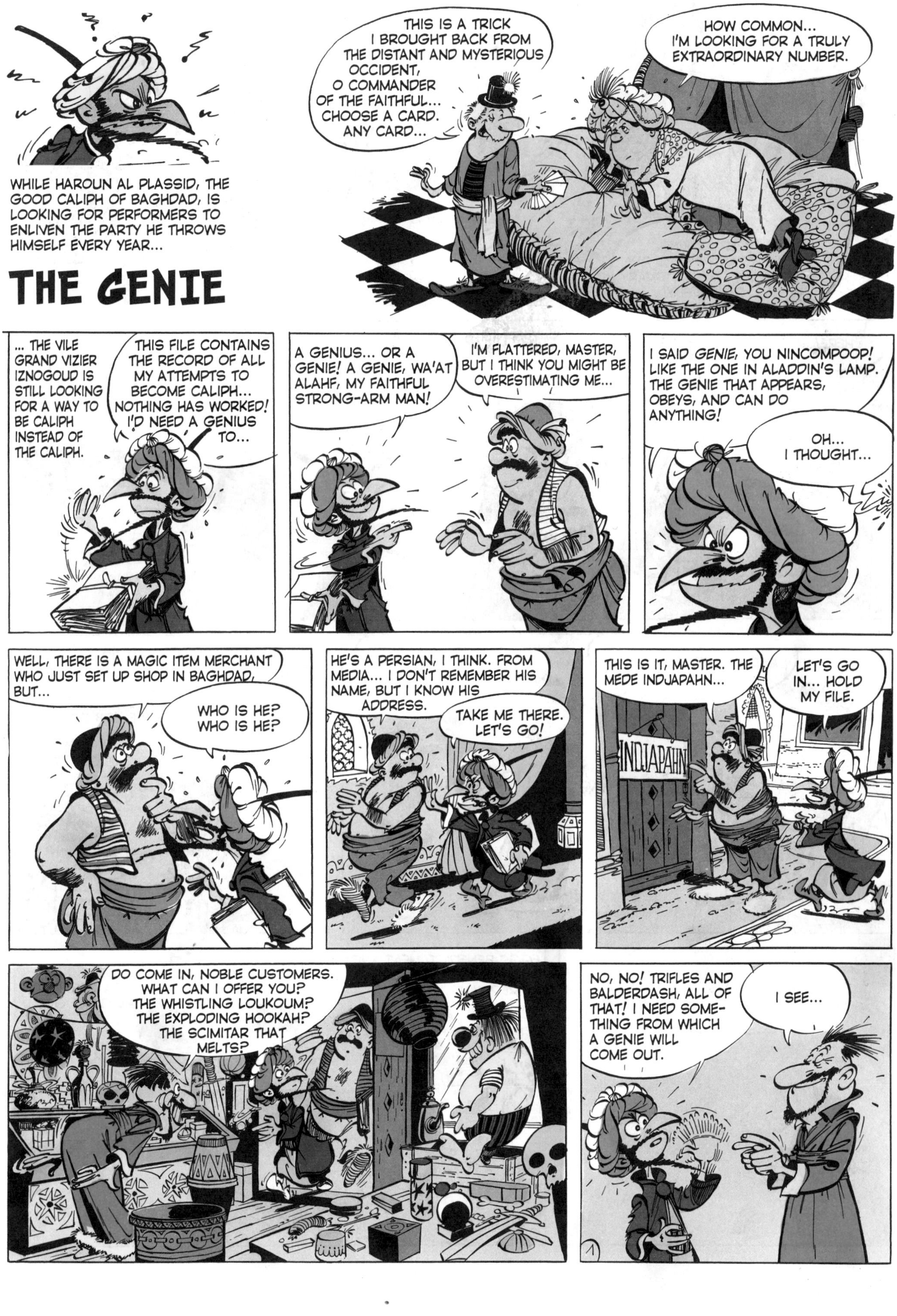

WHILE HAROUN AL PLASSID, THE GOOD CALIPH OF BAGHDAD, IS LOOKING FOR PERFORMERS TO ENLIVEN THE PARTY HE THROWS HIMSELF EVERY YEAR...
THE GENIE
THIS IS A TRICK I BROUGHT BACK FROM THE DISTANT AND MYSTERIOUS OCCIDENT, O COMMANDER OF THE FAITHFUL... CHOOSE A CARD. ANY CARD...
HOW COMMON... I'M LOOKING FOR A TRULY EXTRAORDINARY NUMBER.
... THE VILE GRAND VIZIER IZNOGOUD IS STILL LOOKING FOR A WAY TO BE CALIPH INSTEAD OF THE CALIPH.
THIS FILE CONTAINS THE RECORD OF ALL MY ATTEMPTS TO BECOME CALIPH... NOTHING HAS WORKED! I'D NEED A GENIUS TO...
A GENIUS... OR A GENIE! A GENIE, WA'AT ALAHF, MY FAITHFUL STRONG-ARM MAN!
I'M FLATTERED, MASTER, BUT I THINK YOU MIGHT BE OVERESTIMATING ME...
I SAID GENIE, YOU NINCOMPOOP! LIKE THE ONE IN ALADDIN'S LAMP. THE GENIE THAT APPEARS, OBEYS, AND CAN DO ANYTHING!
OH... I THOUGHT...
WELL, THERE IS A MAGIC ITEM MERCHANT WHO JUST SET UP SHOP IN BAGHDAD, BUT...
WHO IS HE? WHO IS HE?
HE'S A PERSIAN, I THINK. FROM MEDIA... I DON'T REMEMBER HIS NAME, BUT I KNOW HIS ADDRESS.
TAKE ME THERE. LET'S GO!
THIS IS IT, MASTER. THE MEDE INDJAPAHN...
INDJAPAHN
LET'S GO IN... HOLD MY FILE.
DO COME IN, NOBLE CUSTOMERS. WHAT CAN I OFFER YOU? THE WHISTLING LOUKOUM? THE EXPLODING HOOKAH? THE SCIMITAR THAT MELTS?
NO, NO! TRIFLES AND BALDERDASH, ALL OF THAT! I NEED SOMETHING FROM WHICH A GENIE WILL COME OUT.
I SEE...
1

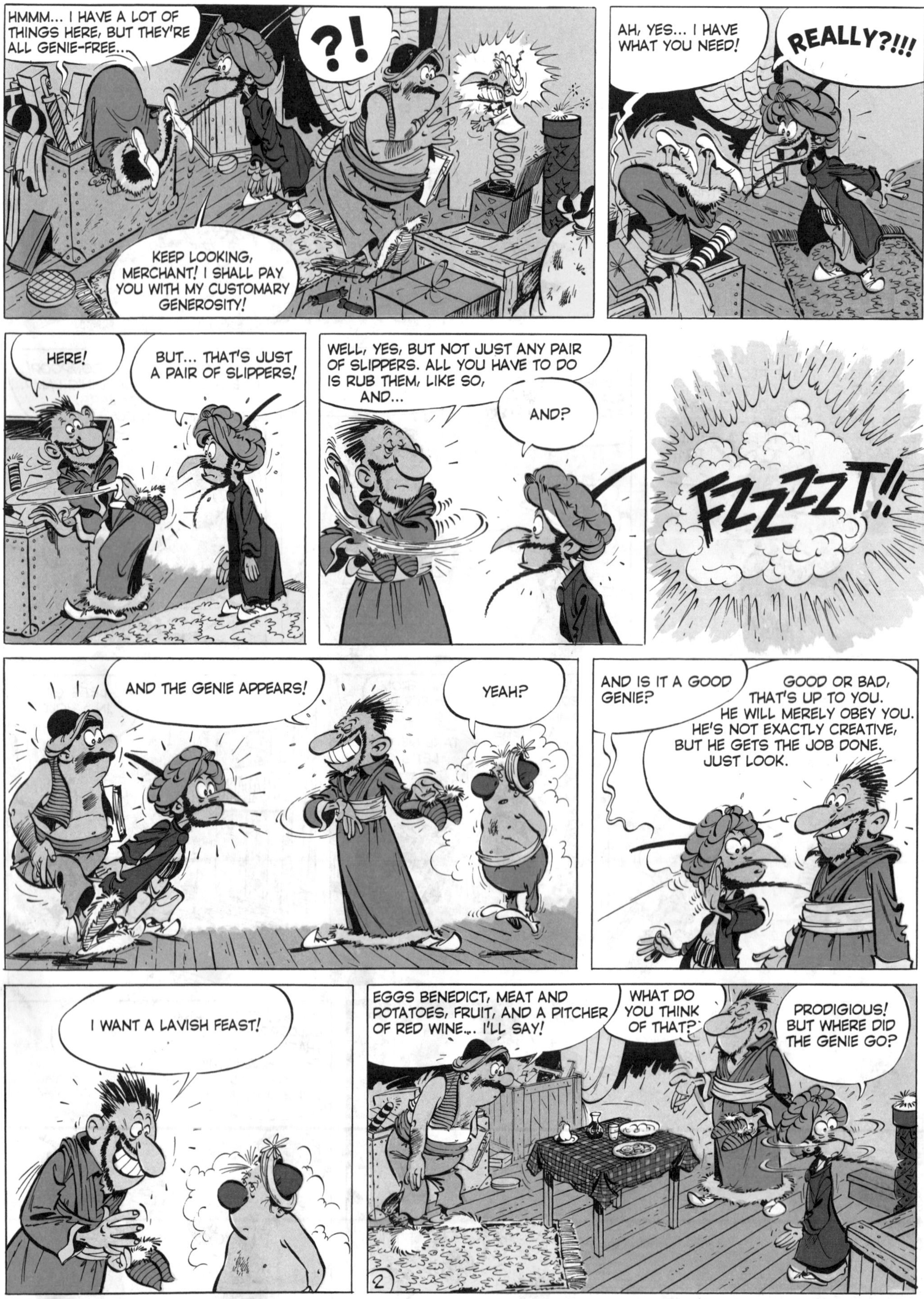
HMMM... I HAVE A LOT OF THINGS HERE, BUT THEY'RE ALL GENIE-FREE...
?!
KEEP LOOKING, MERCHANT! I SHALL PAY YOU WITH MY CUSTOMARY GENEROSITY!
AH, YES... I HAVE WHAT YOU NEED!
REALLY?!!!
HERE!
BUT... THAT'S JUST A PAIR OF SLIPPERS!
WELL, YES, BUT NOT JUST ANY PAIR OF SLIPPERS. ALL YOU HAVE TO DO IS RUB THEM, LIKE SO, AND...
AND?
FZZZZT!!
AND THE GENIE APPEARS!
YEAH?
AND IS IT A GOOD GENIE?
GOOD OR BAD, THAT'S UP TO YOU. HE WILL MERELY OBEY YOU. HE'S NOT EXACTLY CREATIVE, BUT HE GETS THE JOB DONE. JUST LOOK.
I WANT A LAVISH FEAST!
EGGS BENEDICT, MEAT AND POTATOES, FRUIT, AND A PITCHER OF RED WINE... I'LL SAY!
WHAT DO YOU THINK OF THAT?
PRODIGIOUS! BUT WHERE DID THE GENIE GO?

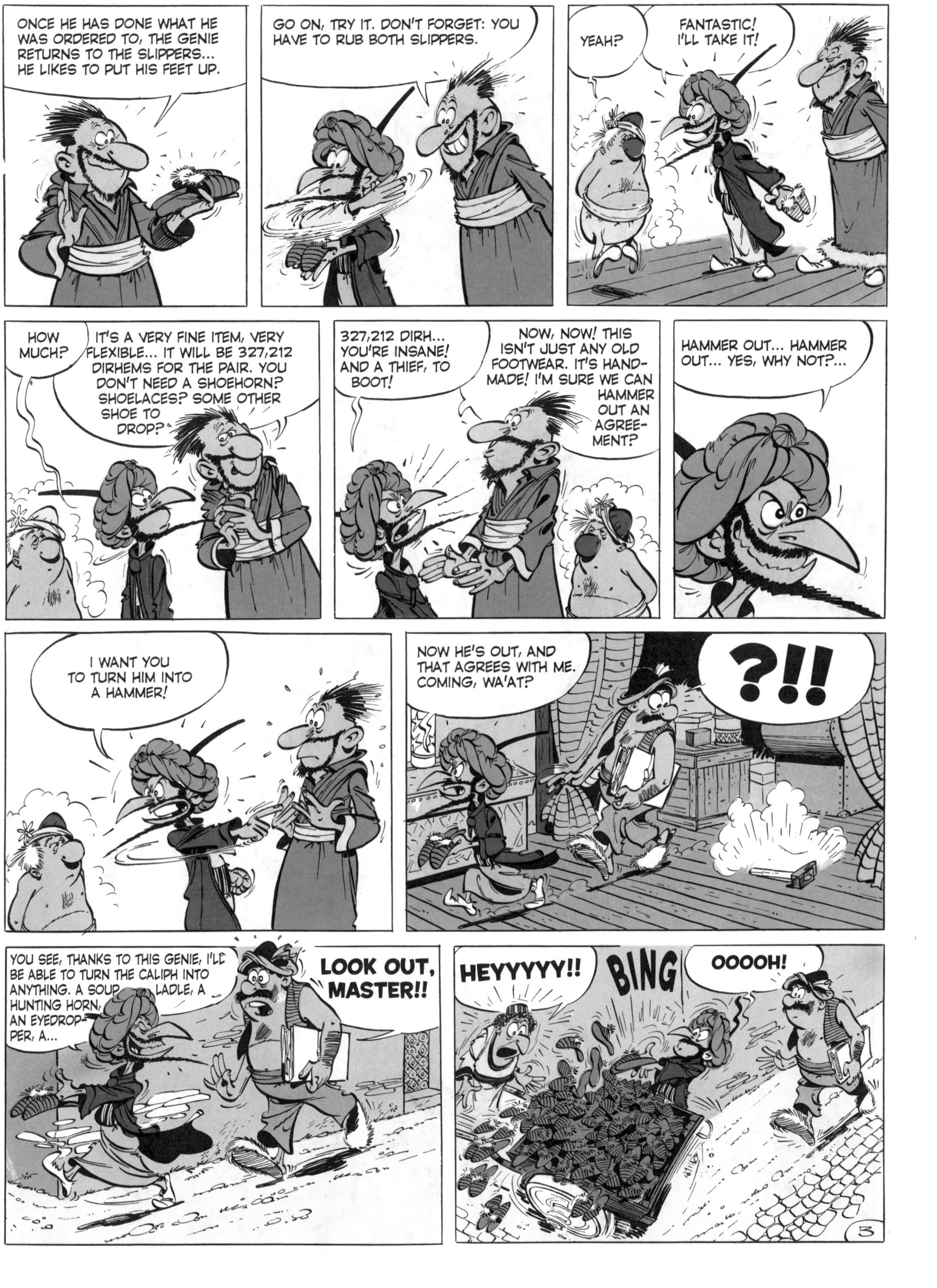
ONCE HE HAS DONE WHAT HE WAS ORDERED TO, THE GENIE RETURNS TO THE SLIPPERS... HE LIKES TO PUT HIS FEET UP.
GO ON, TRY IT. DON'T FORGET: YOU HAVE TO RUB BOTH SLIPPERS.
YEAH?
FANTASTIC! I'LL TAKE IT!
HOW MUCH?
IT'S A VERY FINE ITEM, VERY FLEXIBLE... IT WILL BE 327,212 DIRHEMS FOR THE PAIR. YOU DON'T NEED A SHOEHORN? SHOELACES? SOME OTHER SHOE TO DROP?
327,212 DIRH... YOU'RE INSANE! AND A THIEF, TO BOOT!
NOW, NOW! THIS ISN'T JUST ANY OLD FOOTWEAR. IT'S HAND-MADE! I'M SURE WE CAN HAMMER OUT AN AGREE-MENT?
HAMMER OUT... HAMMER OUT... YES, WHY NOT?...
I WANT YOU TO TURN HIM INTO A HAMMER!
NOW HE'S OUT, AND THAT AGREES WITH ME. COMING, WA'AT?
?!!
YOU SEE, THANKS TO THIS GENIE, I'LL BE ABLE TO TURN THE CALIPH INTO ANYTHING. A SOUP LADLE, A HUNTING HORN, AN EYEDROP-PER, A...
LOOK OUT, MASTER!!
HEYYYYY!!
BING
OOOOH!
3

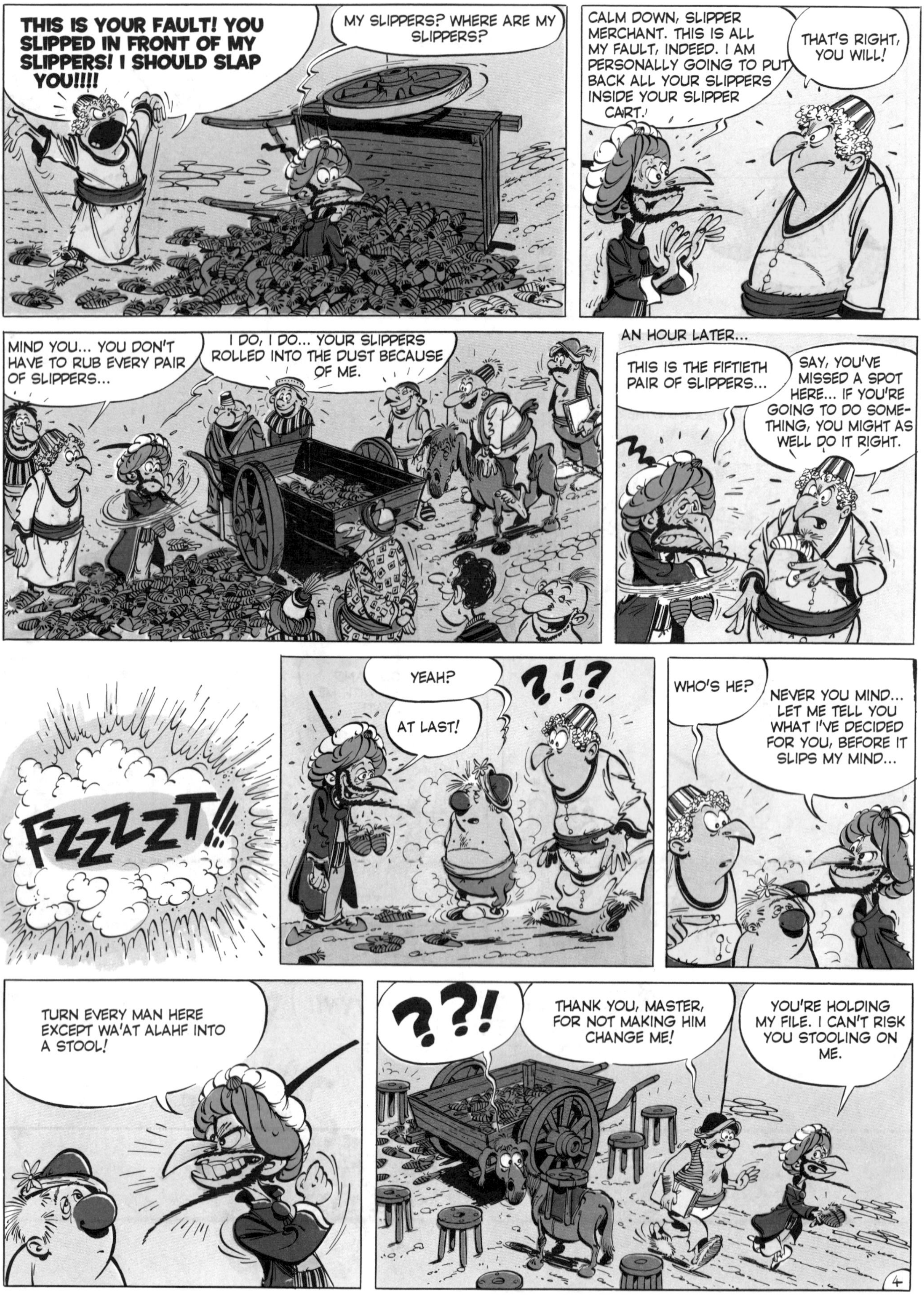

THIS IS YOUR FAULT! YOU SLIPPED IN FRONT OF MY SLIPPERS! I SHOULD SLAP YOU!!!!
MY SLIPPERS? WHERE ARE MY SLIPPERS?
CALM DOWN, SLIPPER MERCHANT. THIS IS ALL MY FAULT, INDEED. I AM PERSONALLY GOING TO PUT BACK ALL YOUR SLIPPERS INSIDE YOUR SLIPPER CART.
THAT'S RIGHT, YOU WILL!
MIND YOU... YOU DON'T HAVE TO RUB EVERY PAIR OF SLIPPERS...
I DO, I DO... YOUR SLIPPERS ROLLED INTO THE DUST BECAUSE OF ME.
AN HOUR LATER...
THIS IS THE FIFTIETH PAIR OF SLIPPERS...
SAY, YOU'VE MISSED A SPOT HERE... IF YOU'RE GOING TO DO SOMETHING, YOU MIGHT AS WELL DO IT RIGHT.
FZZZZT!!!
YEAH?
AT LAST!
?!?
WHO'S HE?
NEVER YOU MIND... LET ME TELL YOU WHAT I'VE DECIDED FOR YOU, BEFORE IT SLIPS MY MIND...
TURN EVERY MAN HERE EXCEPT WA'AT ALAHF INTO A STOOL!
??!
THANK YOU, MASTER, FOR NOT MAKING HIM CHANGE ME!
YOU'RE HOLDING MY FILE. I CAN'T RISK YOU STOOLING ON ME.
4

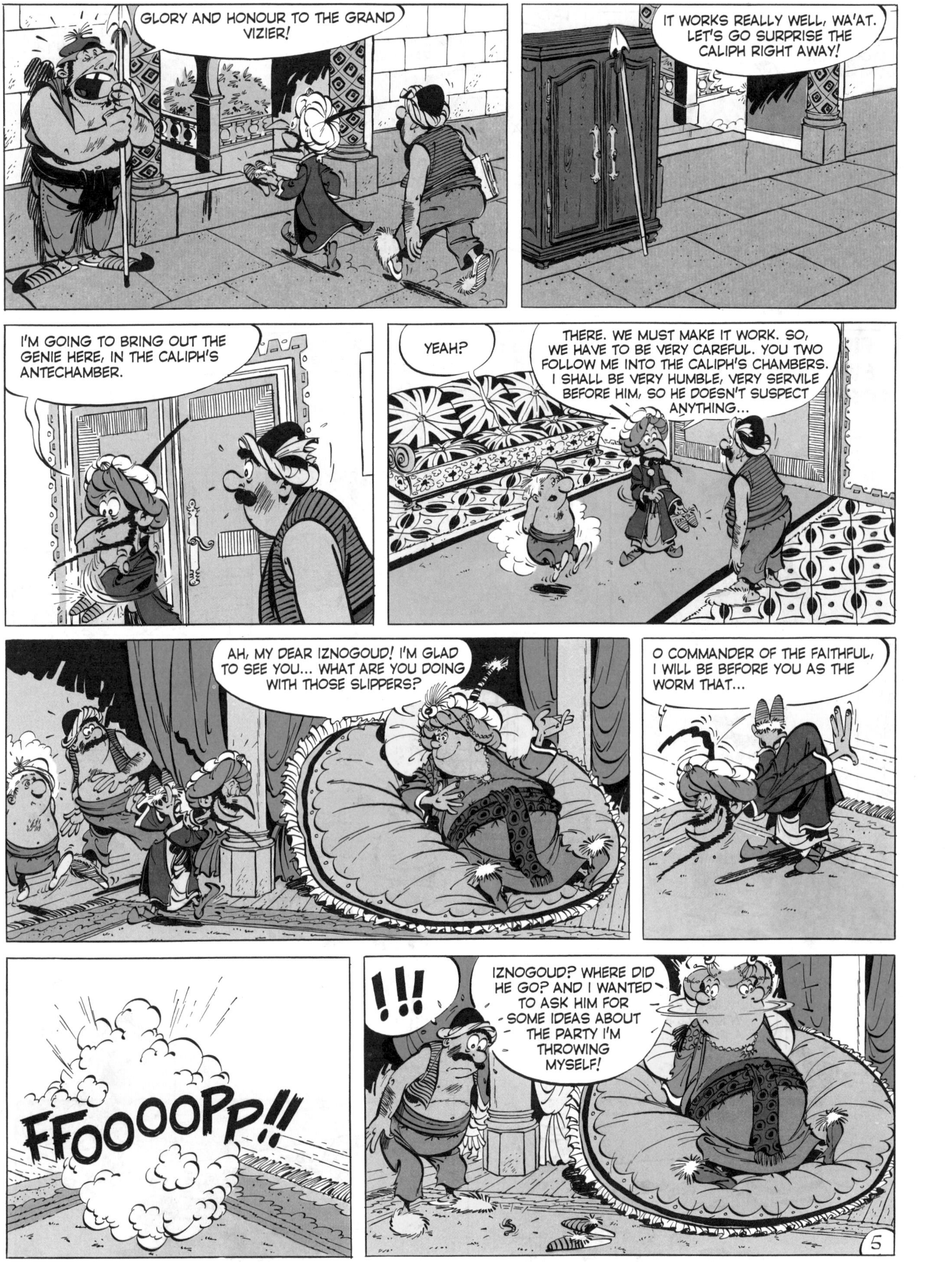
GLORY AND HONOUR TO THE GRAND VIZIER!
IT WORKS REALLY WELL, WA'AT. LET'S GO SURPRISE THE CALIPH RIGHT AWAY!
I'M GOING TO BRING OUT THE GENIE HERE, IN THE CALIPH'S ANTECHAMBER.
YEAH?
THERE. WE MUST MAKE IT WORK. SO, WE HAVE TO BE VERY CAREFUL. YOU TWO FOLLOW ME INTO THE CALIPH'S CHAMBERS. I SHALL BE VERY HUMBLE, VERY SERVILE BEFORE HIM, SO HE DOESN'T SUSPECT ANYTHING...
AH, MY DEAR IZNOGOUD! I'M GLAD TO SEE YOU... WHAT ARE YOU DOING WITH THOSE SLIPPERS?
O COMMANDER OF THE FAITHFUL, I WILL BE BEFORE YOU AS THE WORM THAT...
FFOOOOPP!!
!!!
IZNOGOUD? WHERE DID HE GO? AND I WANTED TO ASK HIM FOR SOME IDEAS ABOUT THE PARTY I'M THROWING MYSELF!
5

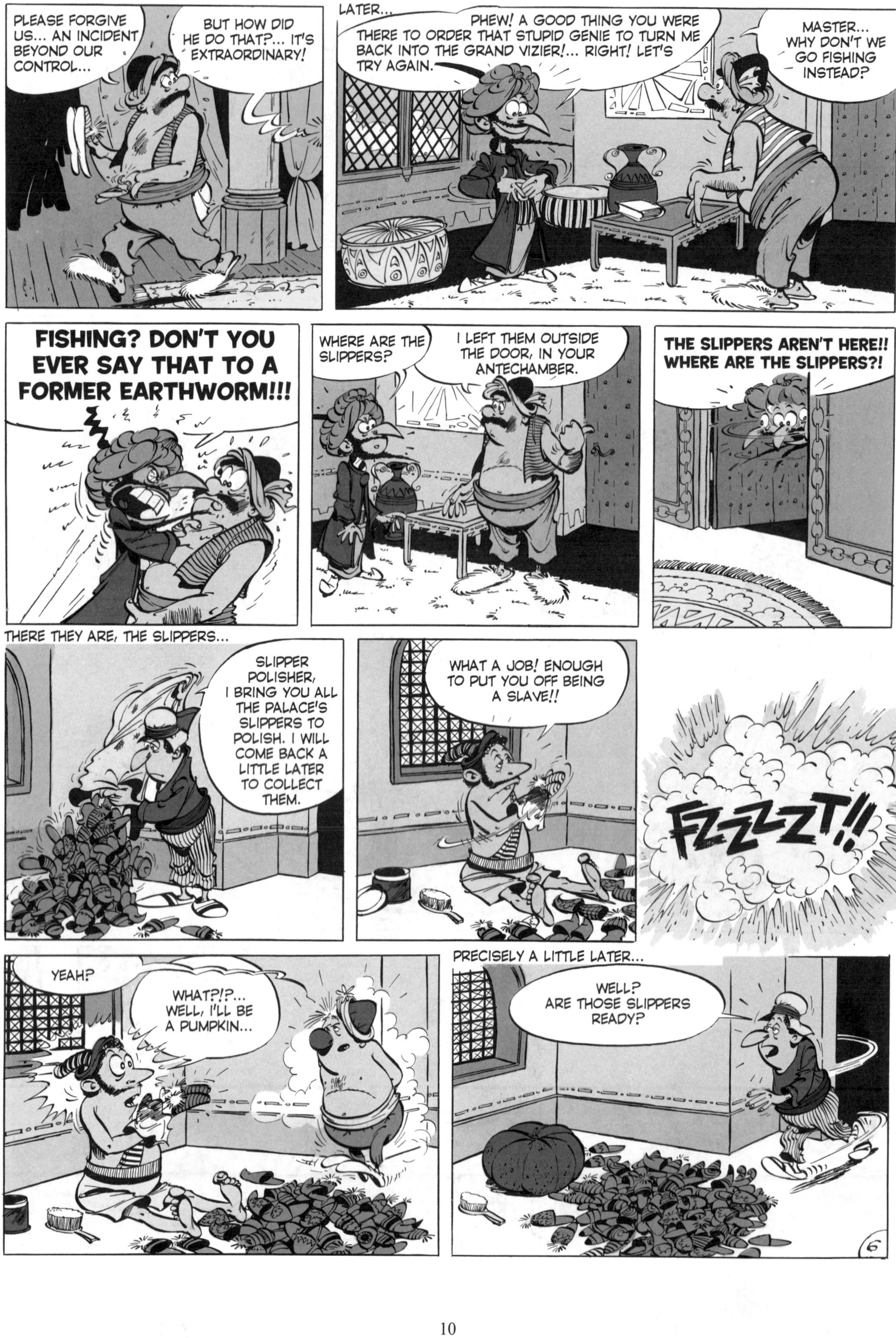
PLEASE FORGIVE US... AN INCIDENT BEYOND OUR CONTROL...
BUT HOW DID HE DO THAT?... IT'S EXTRAORDINARY!
LATER...
PHEW! A GOOD THING YOU WERE THERE TO ORDER THAT STUPID GENIE TO TURN ME BACK INTO THE GRAND VIZIER!... RIGHT! LET'S TRY AGAIN.
MASTER... WHY DON'T WE GO FISHING INSTEAD?
FISHING? DON'T YOU EVER SAY THAT TO A FORMER EARTHWORM!!!
WHERE ARE THE SLIPPERS?
I LEFT THEM OUTSIDE THE DOOR, IN YOUR ANTECHAMBER.
THE SLIPPERS AREN'T HERE!! WHERE ARE THE SLIPPERS?!
THERE THEY ARE, THE SLIPPERS...
SLIPPER POLISHER, I BRING YOU ALL THE PALACE'S SLIPPERS TO POLISH. I WILL COME BACK A LITTLE LATER TO COLLECT THEM.
WHAT A JOB! ENOUGH TO PUT YOU OFF BEING A SLAVE!!
FZZZZT!!
YEAH?
WHAT?!?... WELL, I'LL BE A PUMPKIN...
PRECISELY A LITTLE LATER...
WELL? ARE THOSE SLIPPERS READY?
6

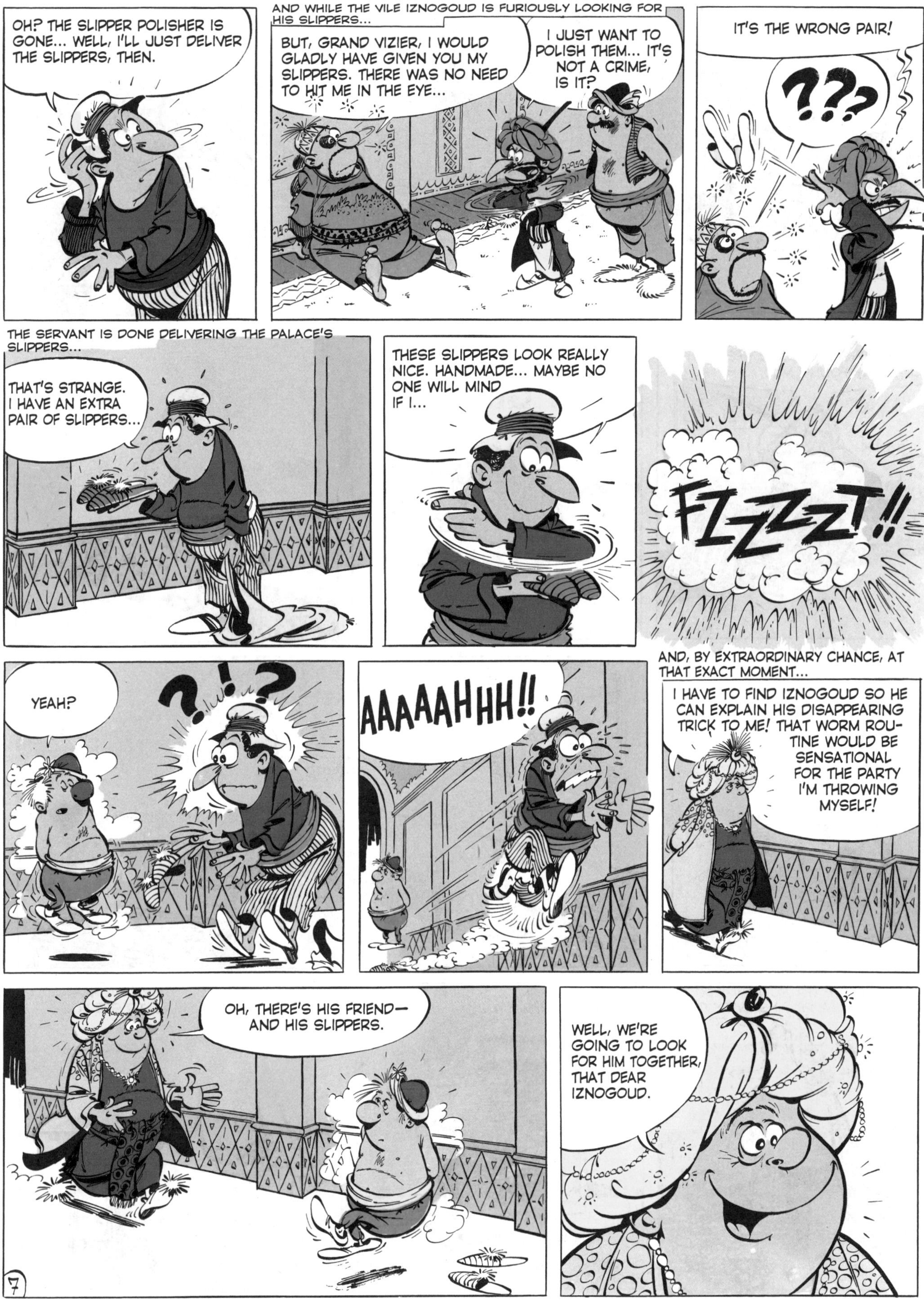
OH? THE SLIPPER POLISHER IS GONE... WELL, I'LL JUST DELIVER THE SLIPPERS, THEN.
AND WHILE THE VILE IZNOGOUD IS FURIOUSLY LOOKING FOR HIS SLIPPERS...
BUT, GRAND VIZIER, I WOULD GLADLY HAVE GIVEN YOU MY SLIPPERS. THERE WAS NO NEED TO HIT ME IN THE EYE...
I JUST WANT TO POLISH THEM... IT'S NOT A CRIME, IS IT?
IT'S THE WRONG PAIR!
???
THE SERVANT IS DONE DELIVERING THE PALACE'S SLIPPERS...
THAT'S STRANGE. I HAVE AN EXTRA PAIR OF SLIPPERS...
THESE SLIPPERS LOOK REALLY NICE. HANDMADE... MAYBE NO ONE WILL MIND IF I...
FZZZZT!!
YEAH?
?!?
AAAAAHHH!!
AND, BY EXTRAORDINARY CHANCE, AT THAT EXACT MOMENT...
I HAVE TO FIND IZNOGOUD SO HE CAN EXPLAIN HIS DISAPPEARING TRICK TO ME! THAT WORM ROUTINE WOULD BE SENSATIONAL FOR THE PARTY I'M THROWING MYSELF!
OH, THERE'S HIS FRIEND— AND HIS SLIPPERS.
WELL, WE'RE GOING TO LOOK FOR HIM TOGETHER, THAT DEAR IZNOGOUD.
7

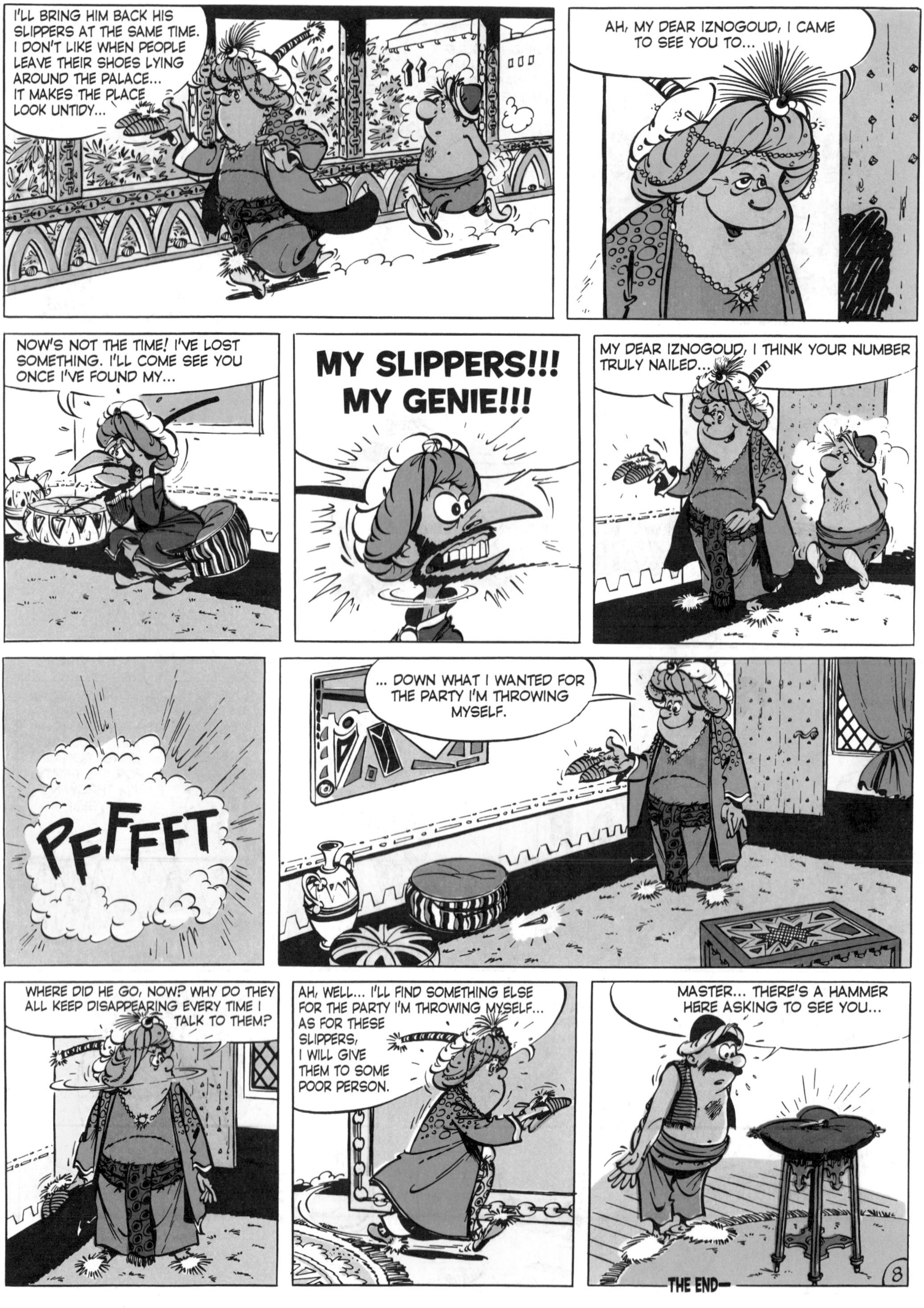

I'LL BRING HIM BACK HIS SLIPPERS AT THE SAME TIME. I DON'T LIKE WHEN PEOPLE LEAVE THEIR SHOES LYING AROUND THE PALACE... IT MAKES THE PLACE LOOK UNTIDY...
AH, MY DEAR IZNOGOUD, I CAME TO SEE YOU TO...
NOW'S NOT THE TIME! I'VE LOST SOMETHING. I'LL COME SEE YOU ONCE I'VE FOUND MY...
MY SLIPPERS!!! MY GENIE!!!
MY DEAR IZNOGOUD, I THINK YOUR NUMBER TRULY NAILED...
PFFFFT
... DOWN WHAT I WANTED FOR THE PARTY I'M THROWING MYSELF.
WHERE DID HE GO, NOW? WHY DO THEY ALL KEEP DISAPPEARING EVERY TIME I TALK TO THEM?
AH, WELL... I'LL FIND SOMETHING ELSE FOR THE PARTY I'M THROWING MYSELF... AS FOR THESE SLIPPERS, I WILL GIVE THEM TO SOME POOR PERSON.
MASTER... THERE'S A HAMMER HERE ASKING TO SEE YOU...
8
THE END

Official Trip

A COURIER COMING FROM ABROAD ENTERS BAGHDAD THE SUMPTUOUS AT A GALLOP, PERCHED ON ONE OF HIS THREE MOUNTS. (COURIERS WOULD BRING SPARE MOUNTS WITH THEM; THIS TYPE OF ROYAL MESSENGER WITH TWO EXTRA HORSES TRAILING BEHIND BELONGED TO THE TRIPLE CROWN CHASE SERVICE).

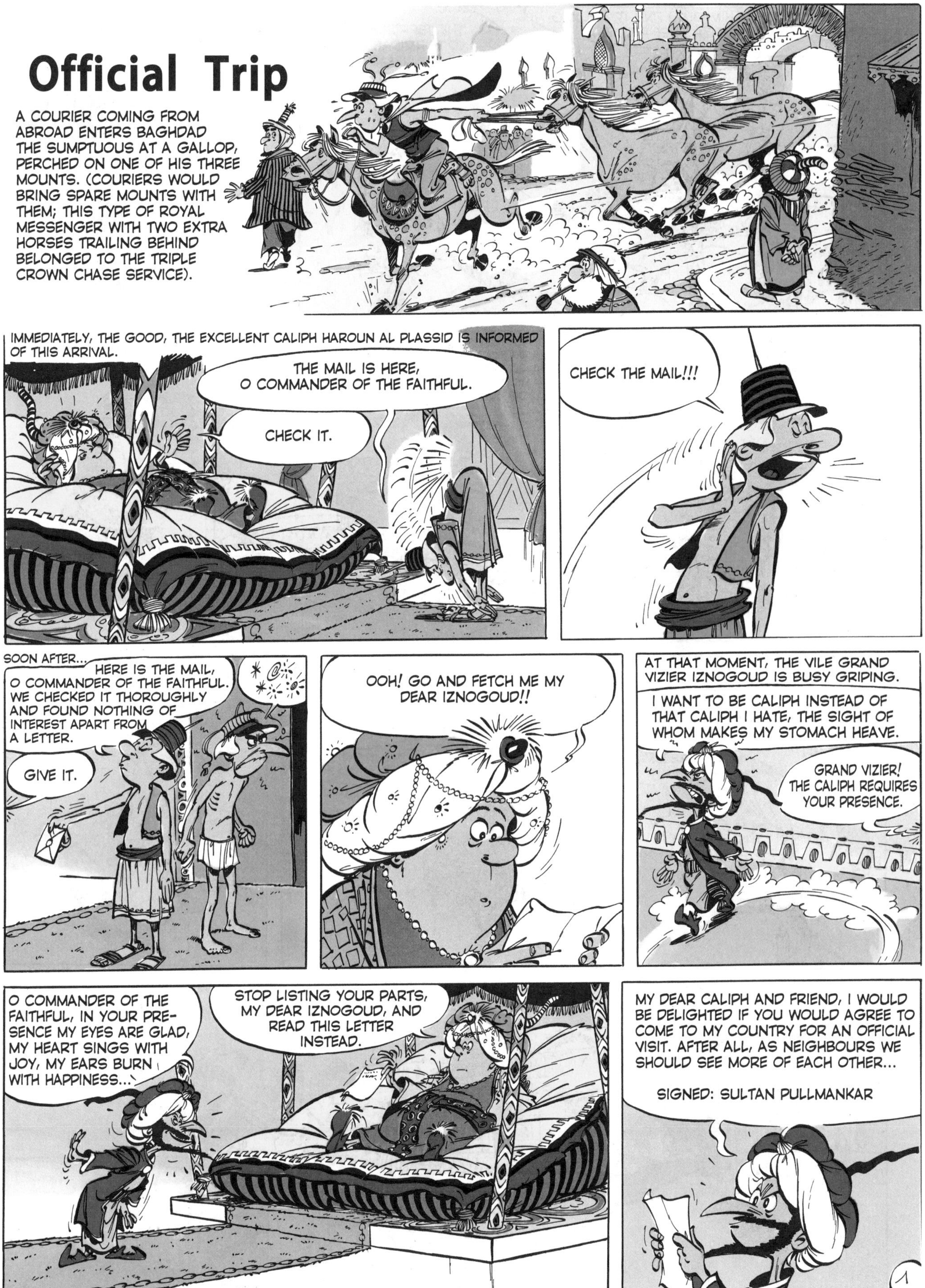

IMMEDIATELY, THE GOOD, THE EXCELLENT CALIPH HAROUN AL PLASSID IS INFORMED OF THIS ARRIVAL.
THE MAIL IS HERE, O COMMANDER OF THE FAITHFUL.
CHECK IT.
CHECK THE MAIL!!!
SOON AFTER...
HERE IS THE MAIL, O COMMANDER OF THE FAITHFUL. WE CHECKED IT THOROUGHLY AND FOUND NOTHING OF INTEREST APART FROM A LETTER.
GIVE IT.
OOH! GO AND FETCH ME MY DEAR IZNOGOUD!!
AT THAT MOMENT, THE VILE GRAND VIZIER IZNOGOUD IS BUSY GRIPING.
I WANT TO BE CALIPH INSTEAD OF THAT CALIPH I HATE, THE SIGHT OF WHOM MAKES MY STOMACH HEAVE.
GRAND VIZIER! THE CALIPH REQUIRES YOUR PRESENCE.
O COMMANDER OF THE FAITHFUL, IN YOUR PRESENCE MY EYES ARE GLAD, MY HEART SINGS WITH JOY, MY EARS BURN WITH HAPPINESS...
STOP LISTING YOUR PARTS, MY DEAR IZNOGOUD, AND READ THIS LETTER INSTEAD.
MY DEAR CALIPH AND FRIEND, I WOULD BE DELIGHTED IF YOU WOULD AGREE TO COME TO MY COUNTRY FOR AN OFFICIAL VISIT. AFTER ALL, AS NEIGHBOURS WE SHOULD SEE MORE OF EACH OTHER...
SIGNED: SULTAN PULLMANKAR
1

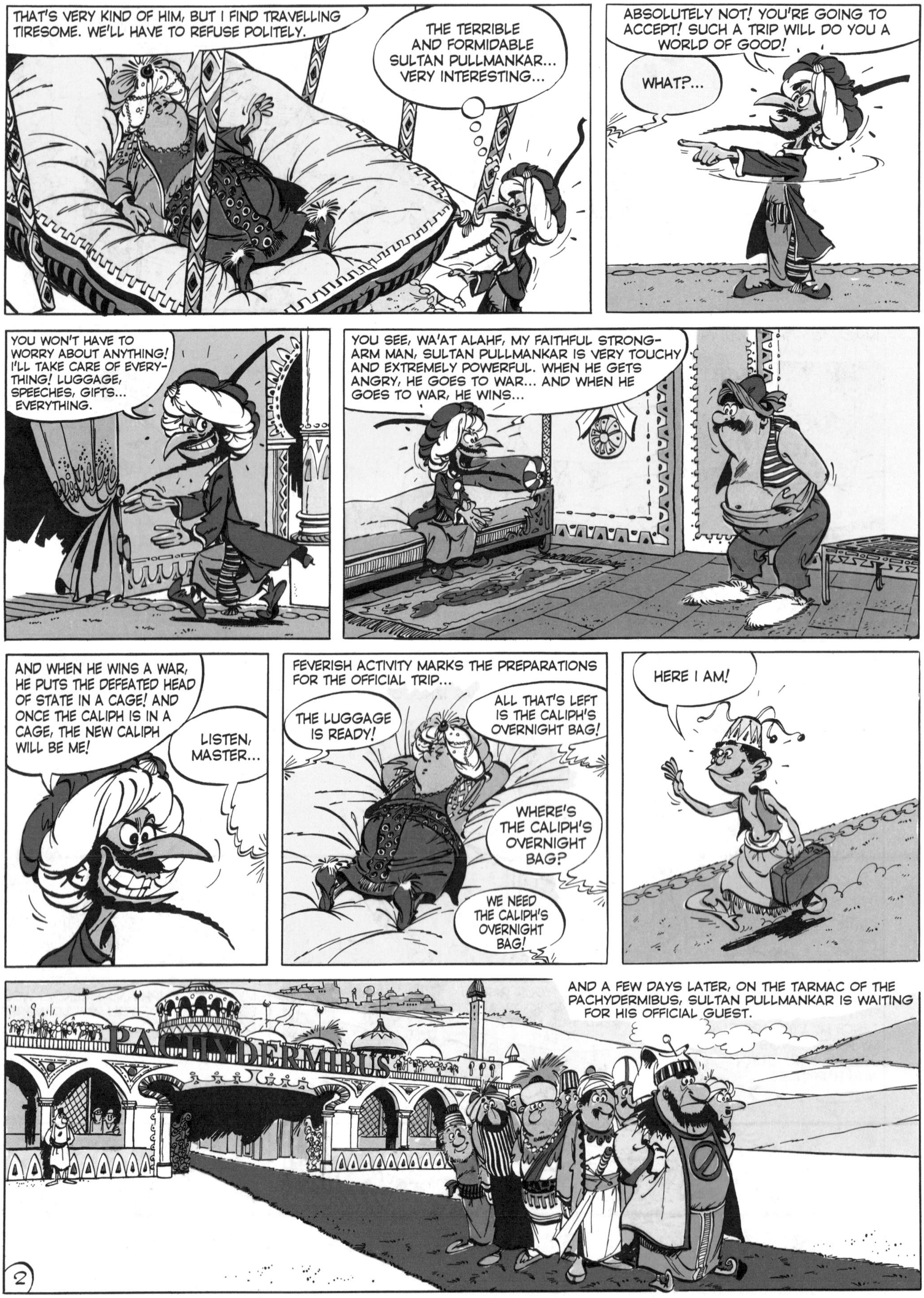
THAT'S VERY KIND OF HIM, BUT I FIND TRAVELLING TIRESOME. WE'LL HAVE TO REFUSE POLITELY.
THE TERRIBLE AND FORMIDABLE SULTAN PULLMANKAR... VERY INTERESTING...
ABSOLUTELY NOT! YOU'RE GOING TO ACCEPT! SUCH A TRIP WILL DO YOU A WORLD OF GOOD!
WHAT?...
YOU WON'T HAVE TO WORRY ABOUT ANYTHING! I'LL TAKE CARE OF EVERYTHING! LUGGAGE, SPEECHES, GIFTS... EVERYTHING.
YOU SEE, WA'AT ALAHF, MY FAITHFUL STRONG-ARM MAN, SULTAN PULLMANKAR IS VERY TOUCHY AND EXTREMELY POWERFUL. WHEN HE GETS ANGRY, HE GOES TO WAR... AND WHEN HE GOES TO WAR, HE WINS...
AND WHEN HE WINS A WAR, HE PUTS THE DEFEATED HEAD OF STATE IN A CAGE! AND ONCE THE CALIPH IS IN A CAGE, THE NEW CALIPH WILL BE ME!
LISTEN, MASTER...
FEVERISH ACTIVITY MARKS THE PREPARATIONS FOR THE OFFICIAL TRIP...
THE LUGGAGE IS READY!
ALL THAT'S LEFT IS THE CALIPH'S OVERNIGHT BAG!
WHERE'S THE CALIPH'S OVERNIGHT BAG?
WE NEED THE CALIPH'S OVERNIGHT BAG!
HERE I AM!
AND A FEW DAYS LATER, ON THE TARMAC OF THE PACHYDERMIBUS, SULTAN PULLMANKAR IS WAITING FOR HIS OFFICIAL GUEST.
PACHYDERMIBUS

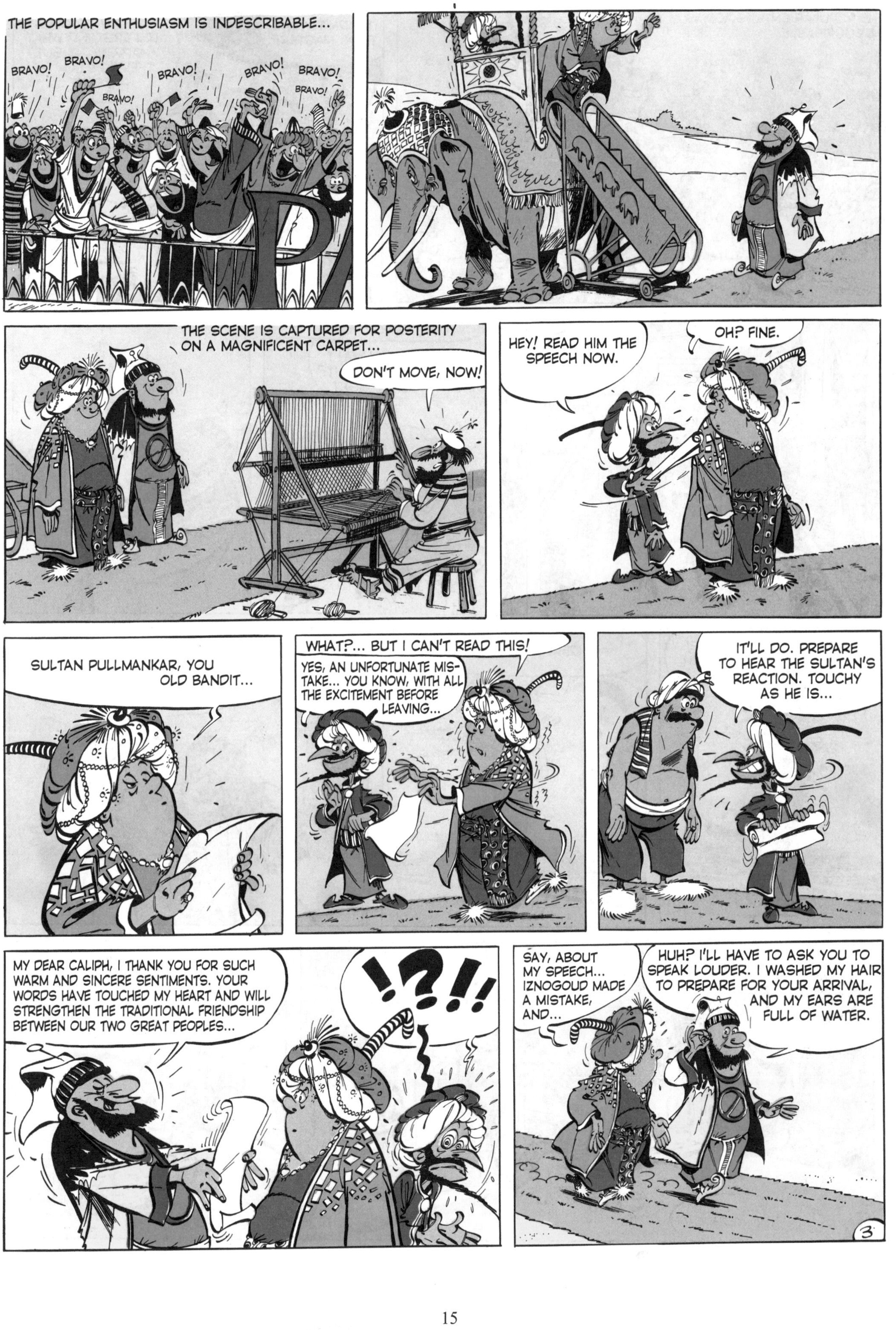
THE POPULAR ENTHUSIASM IS INDESCRIBABLE...
BRAVO!
BRAVO!
BRAVO!
BRAVO!
BRAVO!
BRAVO!
BRAVO!
THE SCENE IS CAPTURED FOR POSTERITY ON A MAGNIFICENT CARPET...
DON'T MOVE, NOW!
HEY! READ HIM THE SPEECH NOW.
OH? FINE.
SULTAN PULLMANKAR, YOU OLD BANDIT...
WHAT?... BUT I CAN'T READ THIS!
YES, AN UNFORTUNATE MISTAKE... YOU KNOW, WITH ALL THE EXCITEMENT BEFORE LEAVING...
IT'LL DO. PREPARE TO HEAR THE SULTAN'S REACTION. TOUCHY AS HE IS...
MY DEAR CALIPH, I THANK YOU FOR SUCH WARM AND SINCERE SENTIMENTS. YOUR WORDS HAVE TOUCHED MY HEART AND WILL STRENGTHEN THE TRADITIONAL FRIENDSHIP BETWEEN OUR TWO GREAT PEOPLES...
!?!!
SAY, ABOUT MY SPEECH... IZNOGOUD MADE A MISTAKE, AND...
HUH? I'LL HAVE TO ASK YOU TO SPEAK LOUDER. I WASHED MY HAIR TO PREPARE FOR YOUR ARRIVAL, AND MY EARS ARE FULL OF WATER.

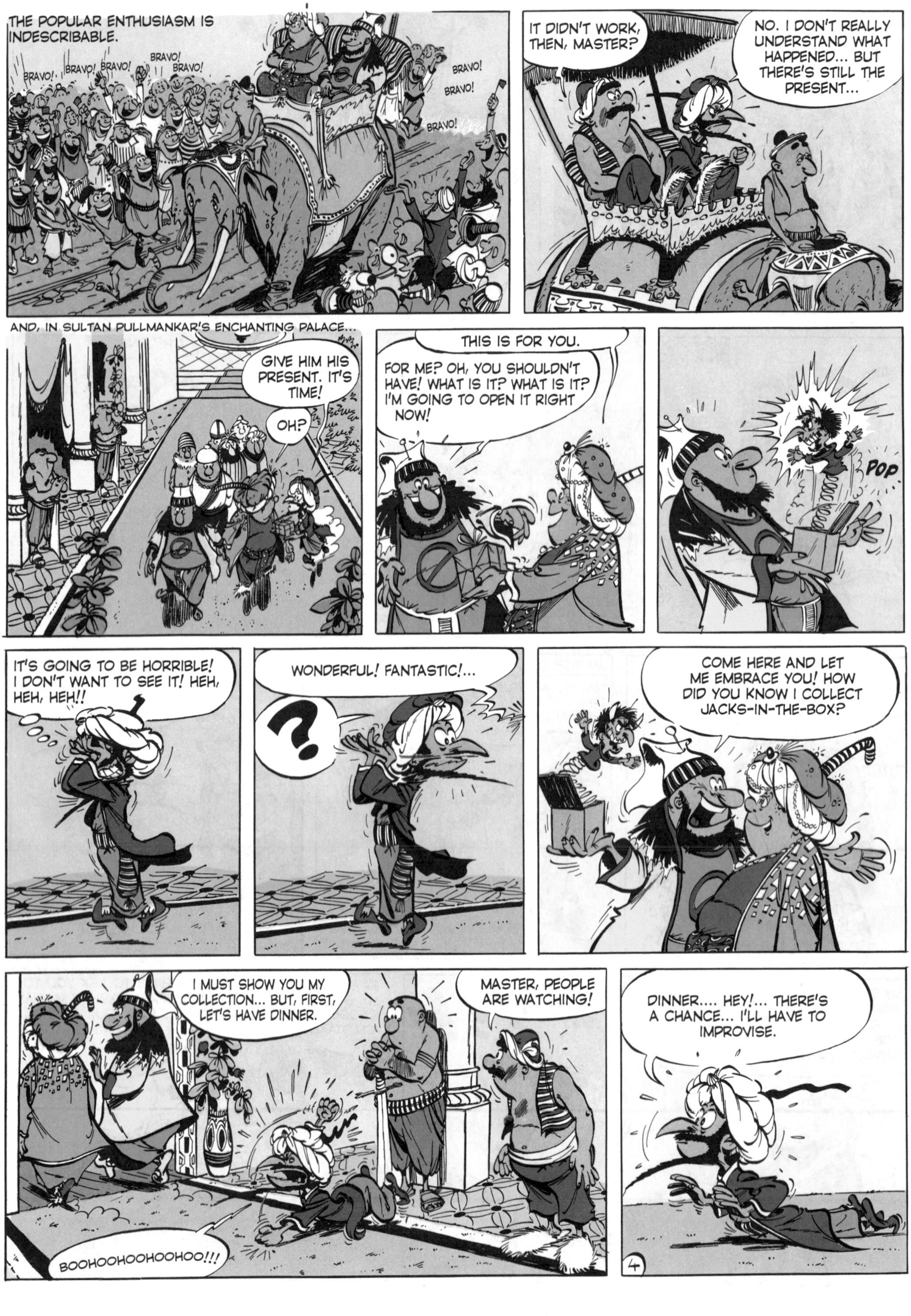
THE POPULAR ENTHUSIASM IS INDESCRIBABLE.
BRAVO! BRAVO! BRAVO! BRAVO! BRAVO!
BRAVO! BRAVO! BRAVO!
IT DIDN'T WORK, THEN, MASTER?
NO. I DON'T REALLY UNDERSTAND WHAT HAPPENED... BUT THERE'S STILL THE PRESENT...
AND, IN SULTAN PULLMANKAR'S ENCHANTING PALACE...
GIVE HIM HIS PRESENT. IT'S TIME!
OH?
THIS IS FOR YOU.
FOR ME? OH, YOU SHOULDN'T HAVE! WHAT IS IT? WHAT IS IT? I'M GOING TO OPEN IT RIGHT NOW!
POP
IT'S GOING TO BE HORRIBLE! I DON'T WANT TO SEE IT! HEH, HEH, HEH!!
WONDERFUL! FANTASTIC!...
?
COME HERE AND LET ME EMBRACE YOU! HOW DID YOU KNOW I COLLECT JACKS-IN-THE-BOX?
I MUST SHOW YOU MY COLLECTION... BUT, FIRST, LET'S HAVE DINNER.
MASTER, PEOPLE ARE WATCHING!
BOOHOOHOOHOOHOO!!!
DINNER.... HEY!... THERE'S A CHANCE... I'LL HAVE TO IMPROVISE.
4

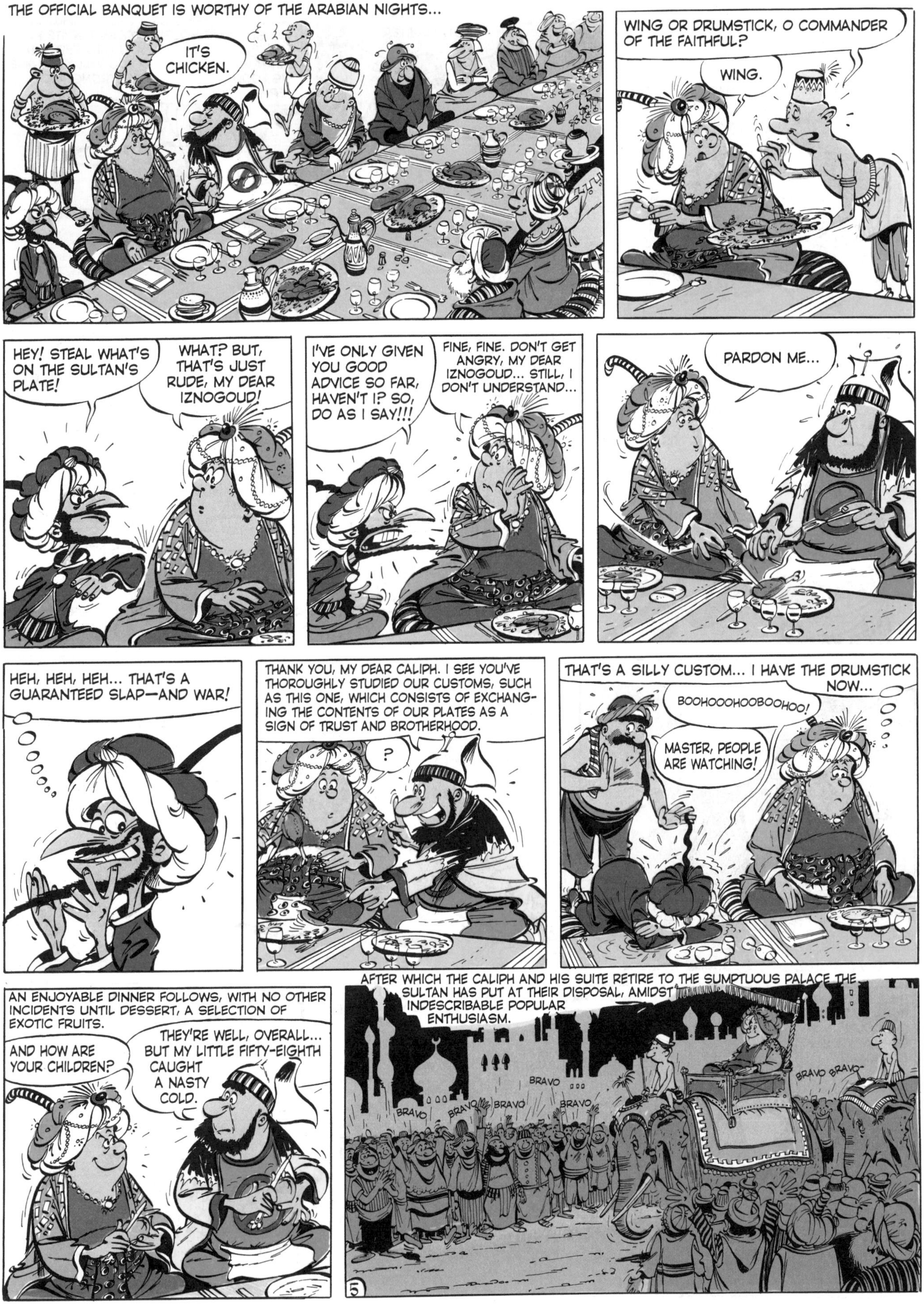
THE OFFICIAL BANQUET IS WORTHY OF THE ARABIAN NIGHTS...
IT'S CHICKEN.
WING OR DRUMSTICK, O COMMANDER OF THE FAITHFUL?
WING.
HEY! STEAL WHAT'S ON THE SULTAN'S PLATE!
WHAT? BUT, THAT'S JUST RUDE, MY DEAR IZNOGOUD!
I'VE ONLY GIVEN YOU GOOD ADVICE SO FAR, HAVEN'T I? SO, DO AS I SAY!!!
FINE, FINE. DON'T GET ANGRY, MY DEAR IZNOGOUD... STILL, I DON'T UNDERSTAND...
PARDON ME...
HEH, HEH, HEH... THAT'S A GUARANTEED SLAP—AND WAR!
THANK YOU, MY DEAR CALIPH. I SEE YOU'VE THOROUGHLY STUDIED OUR CUSTOMS, SUCH AS THIS ONE, WHICH CONSISTS OF EXCHANGING THE CONTENTS OF OUR PLATES AS A SIGN OF TRUST AND BROTHERHOOD.
?
THAT'S A SILLY CUSTOM... I HAVE THE DRUMSTICK NOW...
BOOHOOOHOOBOOHOO!
MASTER, PEOPLE ARE WATCHING!
AN ENJOYABLE DINNER FOLLOWS, WITH NO OTHER INCIDENTS UNTIL DESSERT, A SELECTION OF EXOTIC FRUITS.
AND HOW ARE YOUR CHILDREN?
THEY'RE WELL, OVERALL... BUT MY LITTLE FIFTY-EIGHTH CAUGHT A NASTY COLD.
AFTER WHICH THE CALIPH AND HIS SUITE RETIRE TO THE SUMPTUOUS PALACE THE SULTAN HAS PUT AT THEIR DISPOSAL, AMIDST INDESCRIBABLE POPULAR ENTHUSIASM.
BRAVO
BRAVO BRAVO
BRAVO
BRAVO BRAVO BRAVO
BRAVO BRAVO

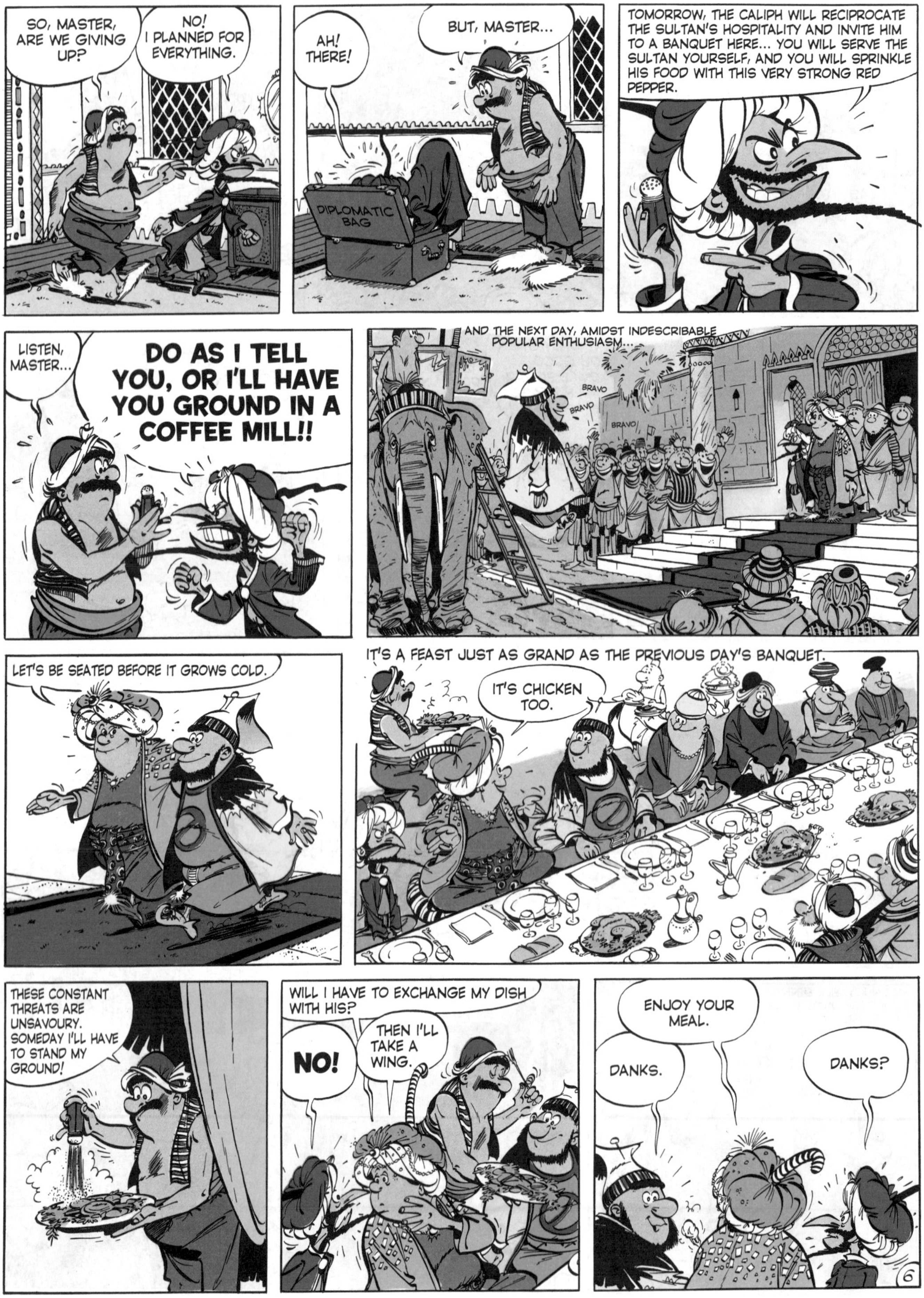
SO, MASTER, ARE WE GIVING UP?
NO! I PLANNED FOR EVERYTHING.
AH! THERE!
BUT, MASTER...
DIPLOMATIC BAG
TOMORROW, THE CALIPH WILL RECIPROCATE THE SULTAN'S HOSPITALITY AND INVITE HIM TO A BANQUET HERE... YOU WILL SERVE THE SULTAN YOURSELF, AND YOU WILL SPRINKLE HIS FOOD WITH THIS VERY STRONG RED PEPPER.
LISTEN, MASTER...
DO AS I TELL YOU, OR I'LL HAVE YOU GROUND IN A COFFEE MILL!!
AND THE NEXT DAY, AMIDST INDESCRIBABLE POPULAR ENTHUSIASM...
BRAVO
BRAVO
BRAVO
LET'S BE SEATED BEFORE IT GROWS COLD.
IT'S A FEAST JUST AS GRAND AS THE PREVIOUS DAY'S BANQUET.
IT'S CHICKEN TOO.
THESE CONSTANT THREATS ARE UNSAVOURY. SOMEDAY I'LL HAVE TO STAND MY GROUND!
WILL I HAVE TO EXCHANGE MY DISH WITH HIS?
NO!
THEN I'LL TAKE A WING.
ENJOY YOUR MEAL.
DANKS.
DANKS?
6

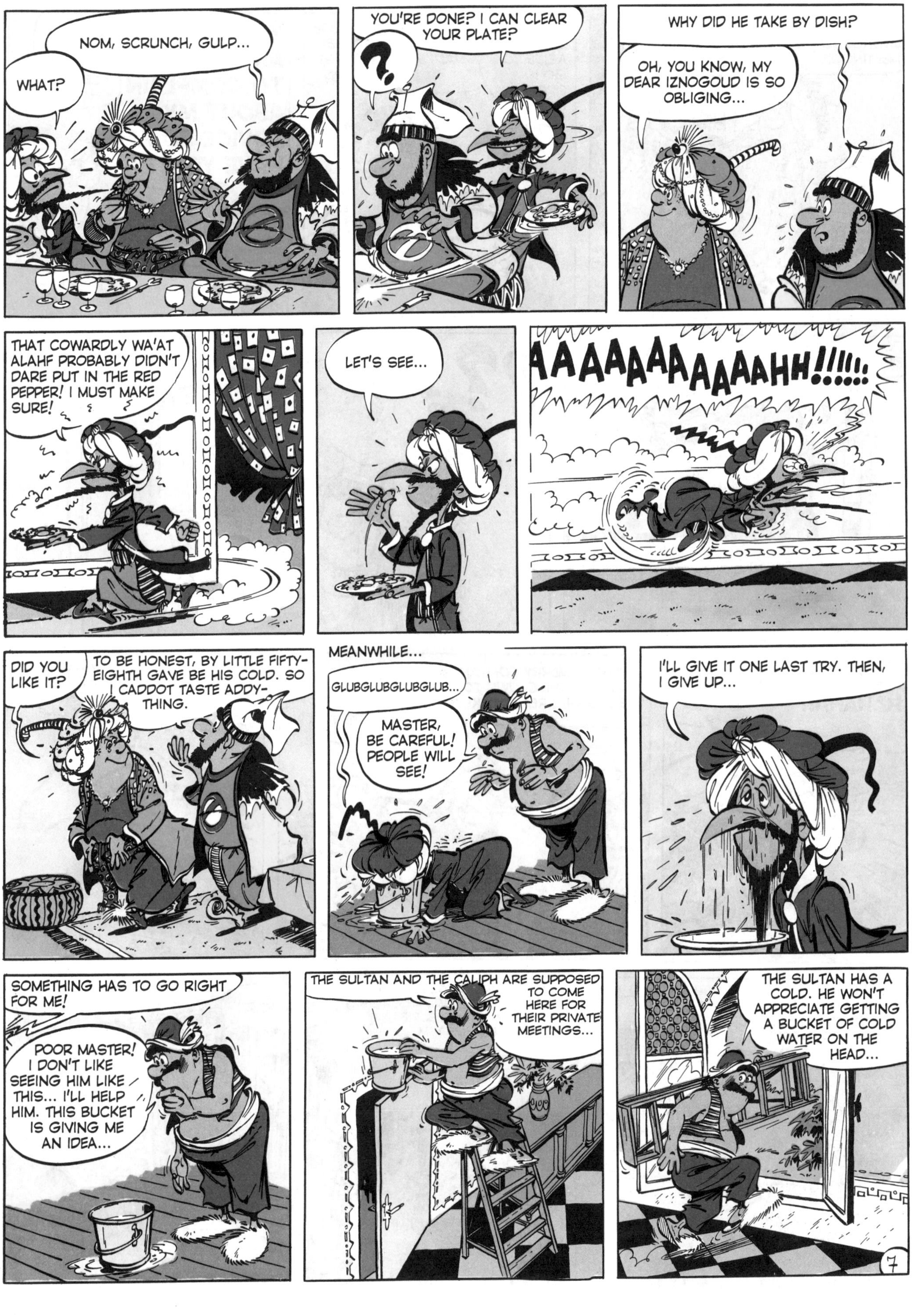
NOM, SCRUNCH, GULP...
WHAT?
YOU'RE DONE? I CAN CLEAR YOUR PLATE?
?
WHY DID HE TAKE BY DISH?
OH, YOU KNOW, MY DEAR IZNOGOUD IS SO OBLIGING...
THAT COWARDLY WA'AT ALAHF PROBABLY DIDN'T DARE PUT IN THE RED PEPPER! I MUST MAKE SURE!
LET'S SEE...
AAAAAAAAAAAAHH!!!!!!
DID YOU LIKE IT?
TO BE HONEST, BY LITTLE FIFTY-EIGHTH GAVE BE HIS COLD. SO I CADDOT TASTE ADDY-THING.
MEANWHILE...
GLUBGLUBGLUBGLUB...
MASTER, BE CAREFUL! PEOPLE WILL SEE!
I'LL GIVE IT ONE LAST TRY. THEN, I GIVE UP...
SOMETHING HAS TO GO RIGHT FOR ME!
POOR MASTER! I DON'T LIKE SEEING HIM LIKE THIS... I'LL HELP HIM. THIS BUCKET IS GIVING ME AN IDEA...
THE SULTAN AND THE CALIPH ARE SUPPOSED TO COME HERE FOR THEIR PRIVATE MEETINGS...
THE SULTAN HAS A COLD. HE WON'T APPRECIATE GETTING A BUCKET OF COLD WATER ON THE HEAD...
7

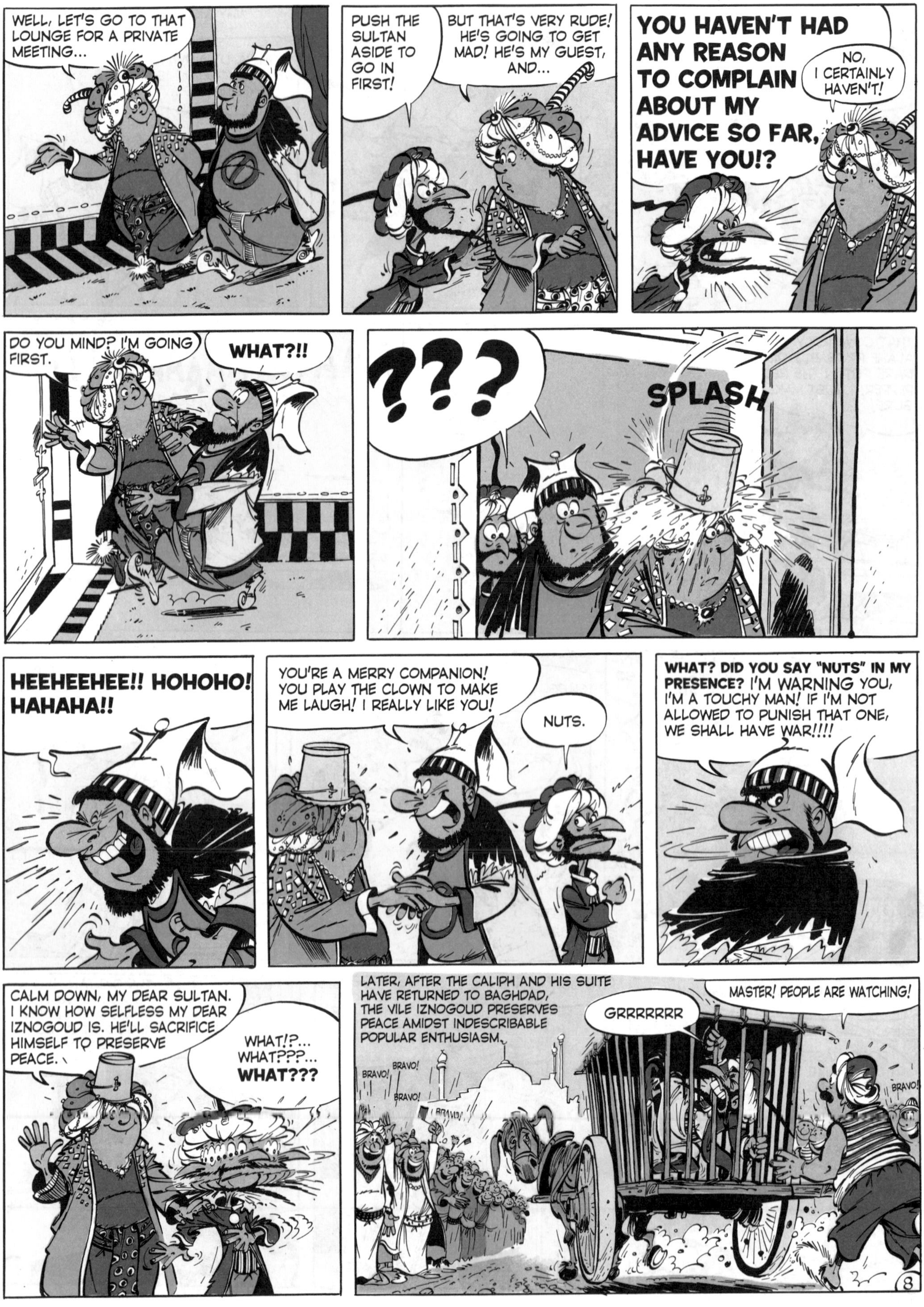
WELL, LET'S GO TO THAT LOUNGE FOR A PRIVATE MEETING...
PUSH THE SULTAN ASIDE TO GO IN FIRST!
BUT THAT'S VERY RUDE! HE'S GOING TO GET MAD! HE'S MY GUEST, AND...
YOU HAVEN'T HAD ANY REASON TO COMPLAIN ABOUT MY ADVICE SO FAR, HAVE YOU!?
NO, I CERTAINLY HAVEN'T!
DO YOU MIND? I'M GOING FIRST.
WHAT?!!
???
SPLASH
HEEHEEHEE!! HOHOHO! HAHAHA!!
YOU'RE A MERRY COMPANION! YOU PLAY THE CLOWN TO MAKE ME LAUGH! I REALLY LIKE YOU!
NUTS.
WHAT? DID YOU SAY "NUTS" IN MY PRESENCE? I'M WARNING YOU, I'M A TOUCHY MAN! IF I'M NOT ALLOWED TO PUNISH THAT ONE, WE SHALL HAVE WAR!!!!
CALM DOWN, MY DEAR SULTAN. I KNOW HOW SELFLESS MY DEAR IZNOGOUD IS. HE'LL SACRIFICE HIMSELF TO PRESERVE PEACE.
WHAT!?... WHAT???... WHAT???
LATER, AFTER THE CALIPH AND HIS SUITE HAVE RETURNED TO BAGHDAD, THE VILE IZNOGOUD PRESERVES PEACE AMIDST INDESCRIBABLE POPULAR ENTHUSIASM.
GRRRRRRR
MASTER! PEOPLE ARE WATCHING!
BRAVO!
BRAVO!
BRAVO!
BRAVO!
BRAVO!
8

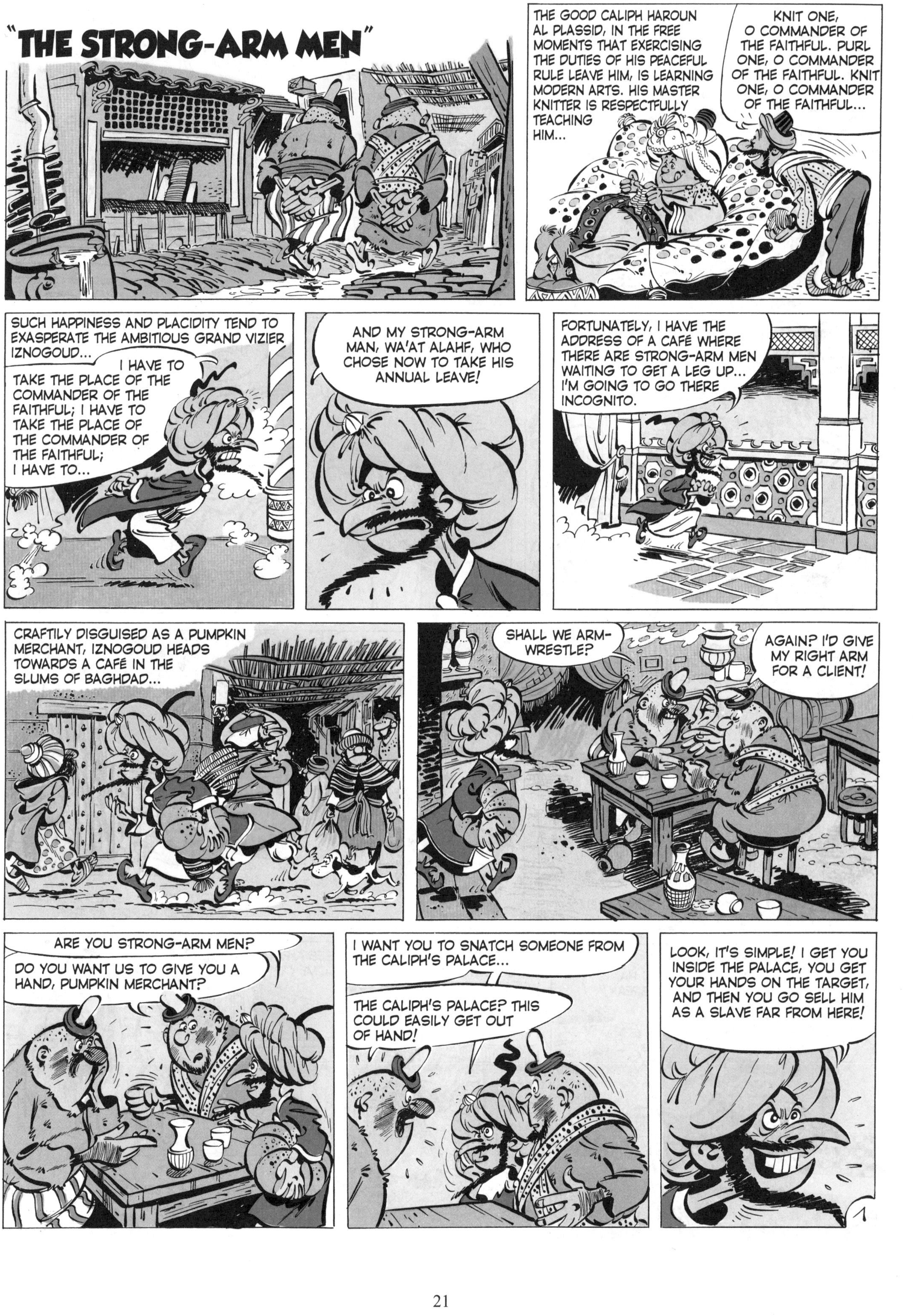
"THE STRONG-ARM MEN"
THE GOOD CALIPH HAROUN AL PLASSID, IN THE FREE MOMENTS THAT EXERCISING THE DUTIES OF HIS PEACEFUL RULE LEAVE HIM, IS LEARNING MODERN ARTS. HIS MASTER KNITTER IS RESPECTFULLY TEACHING HIM...
KNIT ONE, O COMMANDER OF THE FAITHFUL. PURL ONE, O COMMANDER OF THE FAITHFUL. KNIT ONE, O COMMANDER OF THE FAITHFUL...
SUCH HAPPINESS AND PLACIDITY TEND TO EXASPERATE THE AMBITIOUS GRAND VIZIER IZNOGOUD...
I HAVE TO TAKE THE PLACE OF THE COMMANDER OF THE FAITHFUL; I HAVE TO TAKE THE PLACE OF THE COMMANDER OF THE FAITHFUL; I HAVE TO...
AND MY STRONG-ARM MAN, WA'AT ALAHF, WHO CHOSE NOW TO TAKE HIS ANNUAL LEAVE!
FORTUNATELY, I HAVE THE ADDRESS OF A CAFÉ WHERE THERE ARE STRONG-ARM MEN WAITING TO GET A LEG UP... I'M GOING TO GO THERE INCOGNITO.
CRAFTILY DISGUISED AS A PUMPKIN MERCHANT, IZNOGOUD HEADS TOWARDS A CAFÉ IN THE SLUMS OF BAGHDAD...
SHALL WE ARM-WRESTLE?
AGAIN? I'D GIVE MY RIGHT ARM FOR A CLIENT!
ARE YOU STRONG-ARM MEN?
DO YOU WANT US TO GIVE YOU A HAND, PUMPKIN MERCHANT?
I WANT YOU TO SNATCH SOMEONE FROM THE CALIPH'S PALACE...
THE CALIPH'S PALACE? THIS COULD EASILY GET OUT OF HAND!
LOOK, IT'S SIMPLE! I GET YOU INSIDE THE PALACE, YOU GET YOUR HANDS ON THE TARGET, AND THEN YOU GO SELL HIM AS A SLAVE FAR FROM HERE!

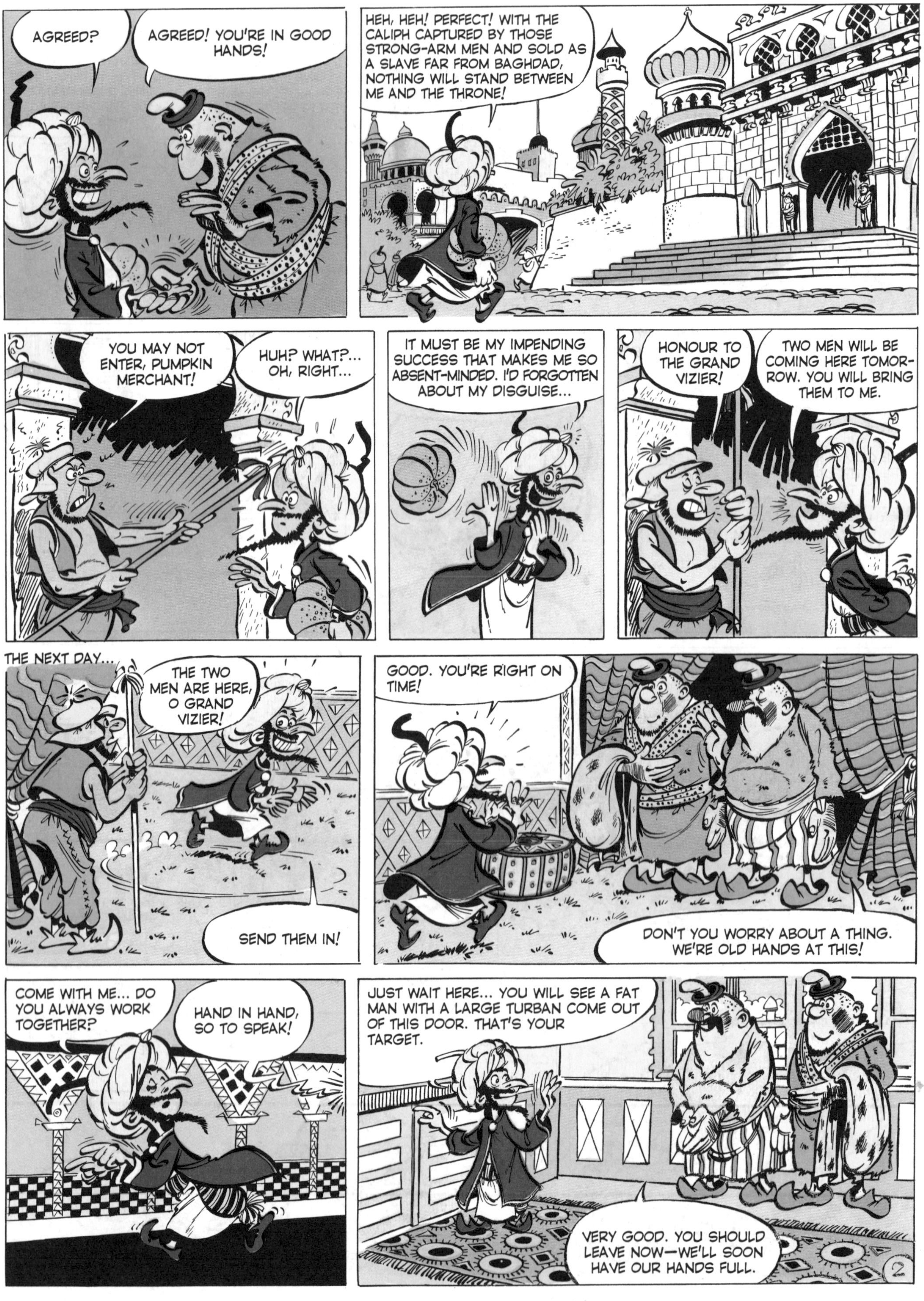
AGREED?
AGREED! YOU'RE IN GOOD HANDS!
HEH, HEH! PERFECT! WITH THE CALIPH CAPTURED BY THOSE STRONG-ARM MEN AND SOLD AS A SLAVE FAR FROM BAGHDAD, NOTHING WILL STAND BETWEEN ME AND THE THRONE!
YOU MAY NOT ENTER, PUMPKIN MERCHANT!
HUH? WHAT?... OH, RIGHT...
IT MUST BE MY IMPENDING SUCCESS THAT MAKES ME SO ABSENT-MINDED. I'D FORGOTTEN ABOUT MY DISGUISE...
HONOUR TO THE GRAND VIZIER!
TWO MEN WILL BE COMING HERE TOMORROW. YOU WILL BRING THEM TO ME.
THE NEXT DAY...
THE TWO MEN ARE HERE, O GRAND VIZIER!
SEND THEM IN!
GOOD. YOU'RE RIGHT ON TIME!
DON'T YOU WORRY ABOUT A THING. WE'RE OLD HANDS AT THIS!
COME WITH ME... DO YOU ALWAYS WORK TOGETHER?
HAND IN HAND, SO TO SPEAK!
JUST WAIT HERE... YOU WILL SEE A FAT MAN WITH A LARGE TURBAN COME OUT OF THIS DOOR. THAT'S YOUR TARGET.
VERY GOOD. YOU SHOULD LEAVE NOW—WE'LL SOON HAVE OUR HANDS FULL.

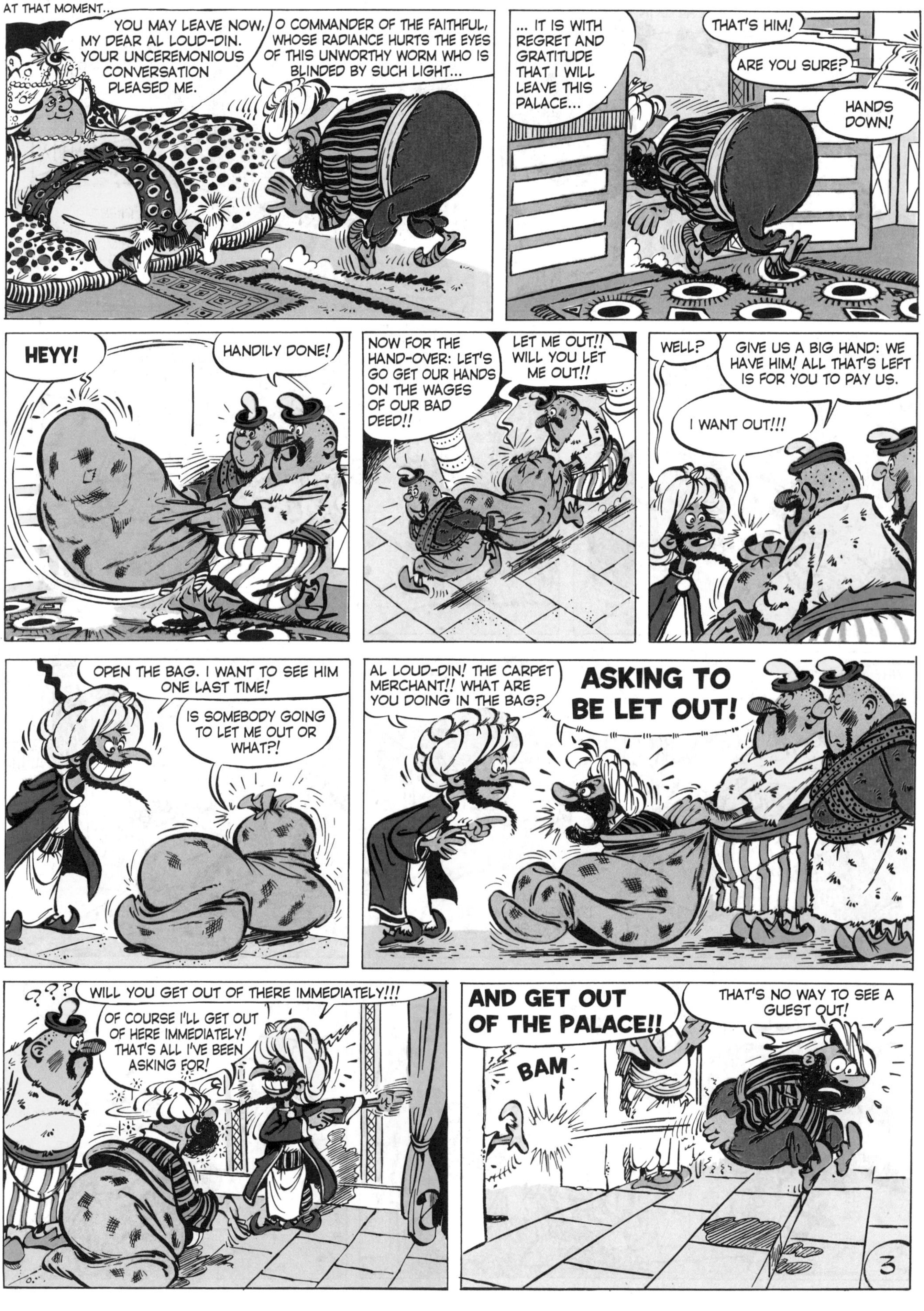
AT THAT MOMENT...
YOU MAY LEAVE NOW, MY DEAR AL LOUD-DIN. YOUR UNCEREMONIOUS CONVERSATION PLEASED ME.
O COMMANDER OF THE FAITHFUL, WHOSE RADIANCE HURTS THE EYES OF THIS UNWORTHY WORM WHO IS BLINDED BY SUCH LIGHT...
... IT IS WITH REGRET AND GRATITUDE THAT I WILL LEAVE THIS PALACE...
THAT'S HIM!
ARE YOU SURE?
HANDS DOWN!
HEYY!
HANDILY DONE!
NOW FOR THE HAND-OVER: LET'S GO GET OUR HANDS ON THE WAGES OF OUR BAD DEED!!
LET ME OUT!! WILL YOU LET ME OUT!!
WELL?
GIVE US A BIG HAND: WE HAVE HIM! ALL THAT'S LEFT IS FOR YOU TO PAY US.
I WANT OUT!!!
OPEN THE BAG. I WANT TO SEE HIM ONE LAST TIME!
IS SOMEBODY GOING TO LET ME OUT OR WHAT?!
AL LOUD-DIN! THE CARPET MERCHANT!! WHAT ARE YOU DOING IN THE BAG?
ASKING TO BE LET OUT!
???
WILL YOU GET OUT OF THERE IMMEDIATELY!!!
OF COURSE I'LL GET OUT OF HERE IMMEDIATELY! THAT'S ALL I'VE BEEN ASKING FOR!
AND GET OUT OF THE PALACE!!
THAT'S NO WAY TO SEE A GUEST OUT!
BAM
3

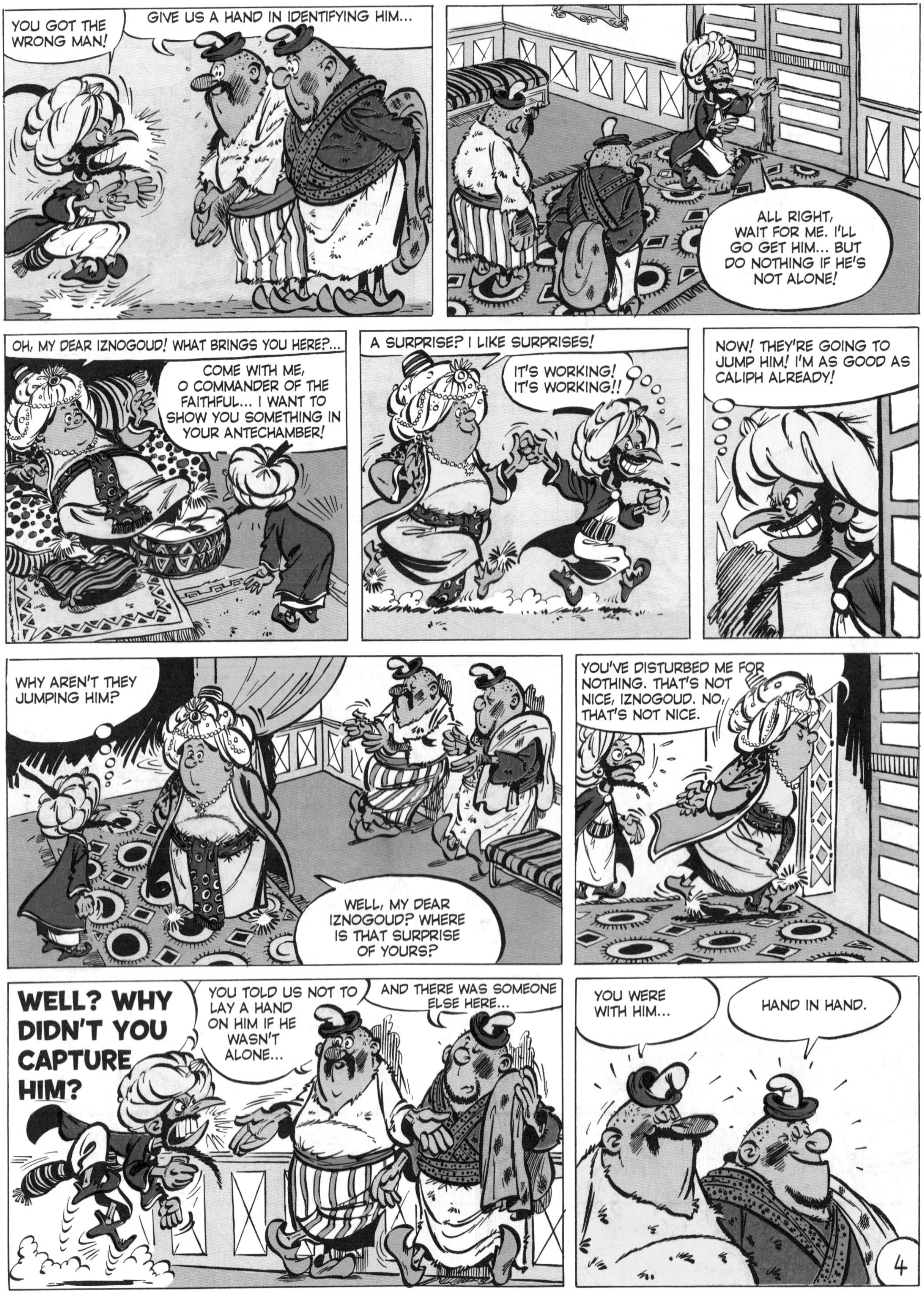
YOU GOT THE WRONG MAN!
GIVE US A HAND IN IDENTIFYING HIM...
ALL RIGHT, WAIT FOR ME. I'LL GO GET HIM... BUT DO NOTHING IF HE'S NOT ALONE!
OH, MY DEAR IZNOGOUD! WHAT BRINGS YOU HERE?...
COME WITH ME, O COMMANDER OF THE FAITHFUL... I WANT TO SHOW YOU SOMETHING IN YOUR ANTECHAMBER!
A SURPRISE? I LIKE SURPRISES!
IT'S WORKING! IT'S WORKING!!
NOW! THEY'RE GOING TO JUMP HIM! I'M AS GOOD AS CALIPH ALREADY!
WHY AREN'T THEY JUMPING HIM?
WELL, MY DEAR IZNOGOUD? WHERE IS THAT SURPRISE OF YOURS?
YOU'VE DISTURBED ME FOR NOTHING. THAT'S NOT NICE, IZNOGOUD. NO, THAT'S NOT NICE.
WELL? WHY DIDN'T YOU CAPTURE HIM?
YOU TOLD US NOT TO LAY A HAND ON HIM IF HE WASN'T ALONE...
AND THERE WAS SOMEONE ELSE HERE...
YOU WERE WITH HIM...
HAND IN HAND.
4

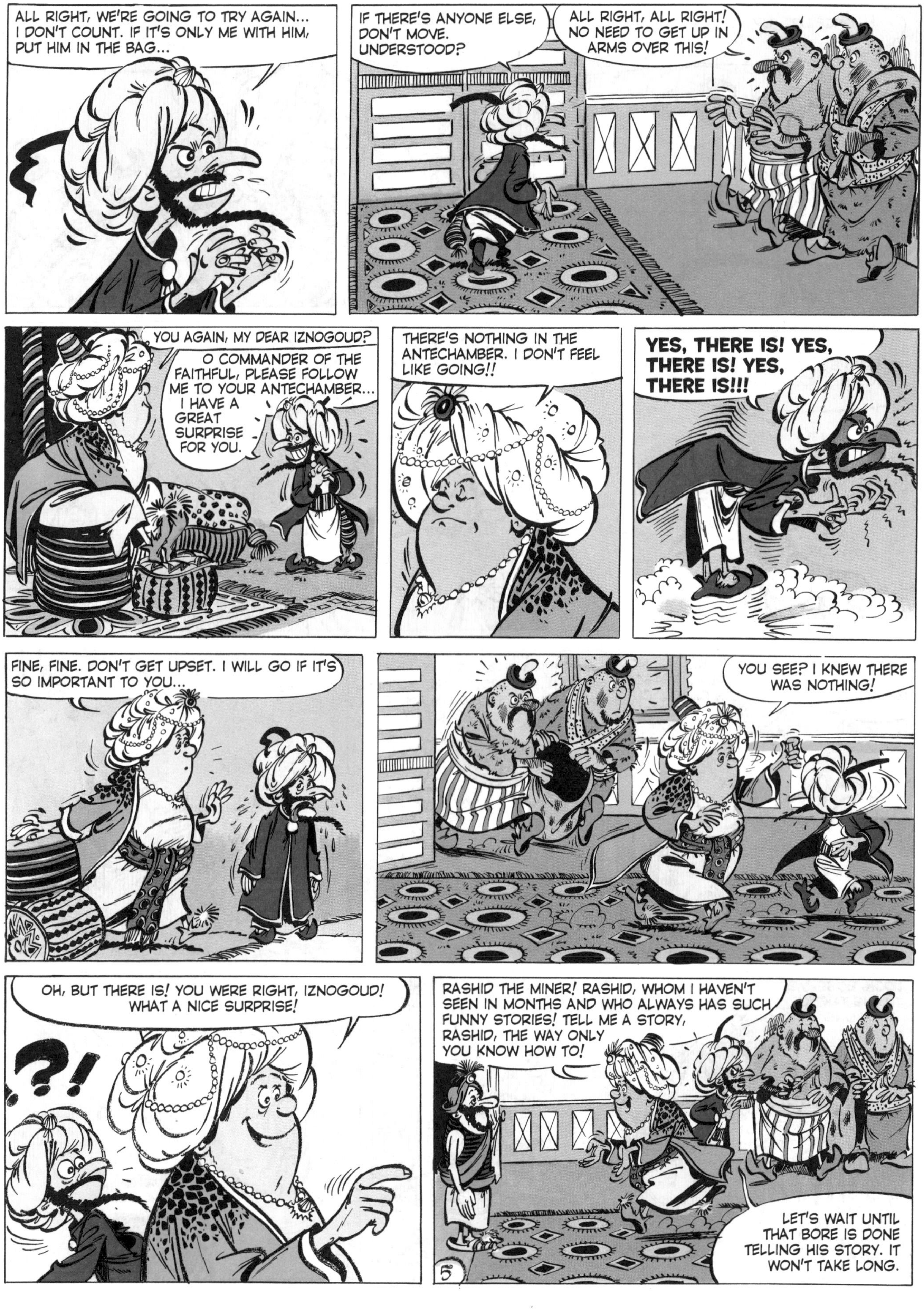
ALL RIGHT, WE'RE GOING TO TRY AGAIN... I DON'T COUNT. IF IT'S ONLY ME WITH HIM, PUT HIM IN THE BAG...
IF THERE'S ANYONE ELSE, DON'T MOVE. UNDERSTOOD?
ALL RIGHT, ALL RIGHT! NO NEED TO GET UP IN ARMS OVER THIS!
YOU AGAIN, MY DEAR IZNOGOUD?
O COMMANDER OF THE FAITHFUL, PLEASE FOLLOW ME TO YOUR ANTECHAMBER... I HAVE A GREAT SURPRISE FOR YOU.
THERE'S NOTHING IN THE ANTECHAMBER. I DON'T FEEL LIKE GOING!!
YES, THERE IS! YES, THERE IS! YES, THERE IS!!!
FINE, FINE. DON'T GET UPSET. I WILL GO IF IT'S SO IMPORTANT TO YOU...
YOU SEE? I KNEW THERE WAS NOTHING!
OH, BUT THERE IS! YOU WERE RIGHT, IZNOGOUD! WHAT A NICE SURPRISE!
.?!
RASHID THE MINER! RASHID, WHOM I HAVEN'T SEEN IN MONTHS AND WHO ALWAYS HAS SUCH FUNNY STORIES! TELL ME A STORY, RASHID, THE WAY ONLY YOU KNOW HOW TO!
LET'S WAIT UNTIL THAT BORE IS DONE TELLING HIS STORY. IT WON'T TAKE LONG.
5

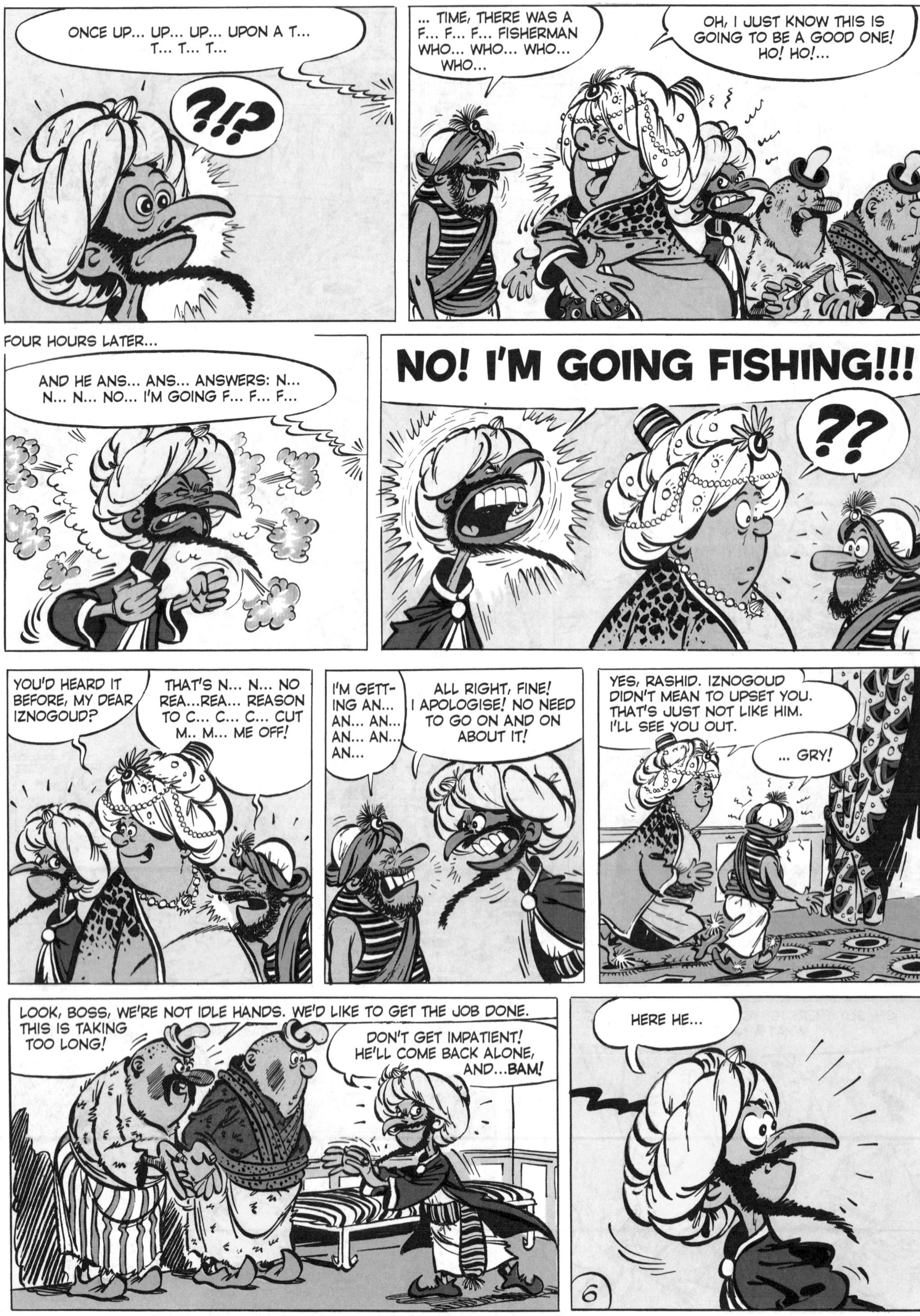
ONCE UP... UP... UP... UPON A T... T... T... T...
?!?
... TIME, THERE WAS A F... F... F... FISHERMAN WHO... WHO... WHO... WHO...
OH, I JUST KNOW THIS IS GOING TO BE A GOOD ONE! HO! HO!...
FOUR HOURS LATER...
AND HE ANS... ANS... ANSWERS: N... N... N... NO... I'M GOING F... F... F...
NO! I'M GOING FISHING!!!
??
YOU'D HEARD IT BEFORE, MY DEAR IZNOGOUD?
THAT'S N... N... NO REA...REA... REASON TO C... C... C... CUT M.. M... ME OFF!
I'M GETT-ING AN... AN... AN... AN... AN... AN...
ALL RIGHT, FINE! I APOLOGISE! NO NEED TO GO ON AND ON ABOUT IT!
YES, RASHID. IZNOGOUD DIDN'T MEAN TO UPSET YOU. THAT'S JUST NOT LIKE HIM. I'LL SEE YOU OUT.
... GRY!
LOOK, BOSS, WE'RE NOT IDLE HANDS. WE'D LIKE TO GET THE JOB DONE. THIS IS TAKING TOO LONG!
DON'T GET IMPATIENT! HE'LL COME BACK ALONE, AND...BAM!
HERE HE...
6

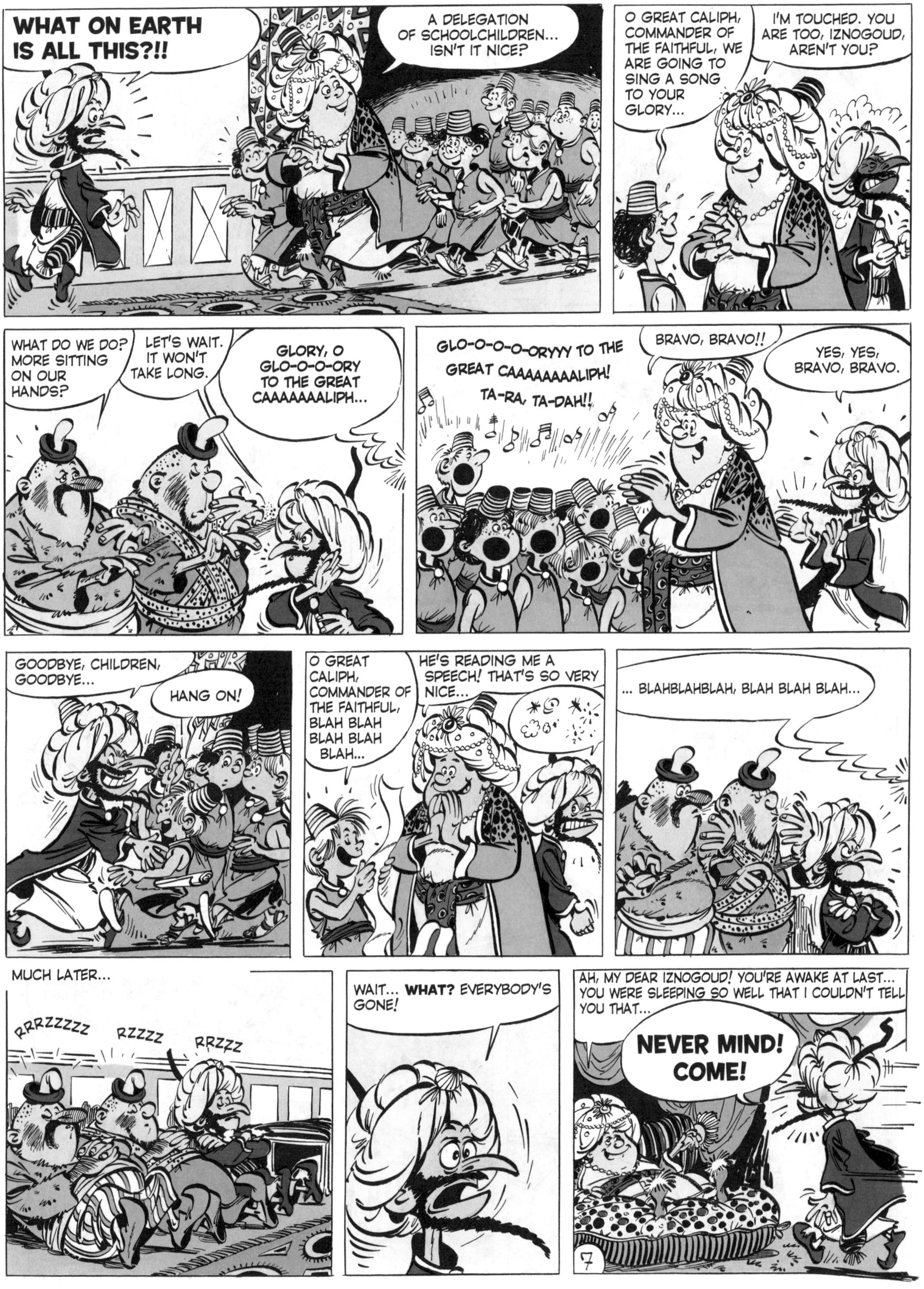
WHAT ON EARTH IS ALL THIS?!!
A DELEGATION OF SCHOOLCHILDREN... ISN'T IT NICE?
O GREAT CALIPH, COMMANDER OF THE FAITHFUL, WE ARE GOING TO SING A SONG TO YOUR GLORY...
I'M TOUCHED. YOU ARE TOO, IZNOGOUD, AREN'T YOU?
WHAT DO WE DO? MORE SITTING ON OUR HANDS?
LET'S WAIT. IT WON'T TAKE LONG.
GLORY, O GLO-O-O-ORY TO THE GREAT CAAAAAAALIPH...
GLO-O-O-O-ORYYY TO THE GREAT CAAAAAAAALIPH! TA-RA, TA-DAH!!
BRAVO, BRAVO!!
YES, YES, BRAVO, BRAVO.
GOODBYE, CHILDREN, GOODBYE...
HANG ON!
O GREAT CALIPH, COMMANDER OF THE FAITHFUL, BLAH BLAH BLAH BLAH BLAH...
HE'S READING ME A SPEECH! THAT'S SO VERY NICE...
... BLAHBLAHBLAH, BLAH BLAH BLAH...
MUCH LATER...
RRRZZZZZ
RZZZZ
RRZZZ
WAIT... WHAT? EVERYBODY'S GONE!
AH, MY DEAR IZNOGOUD! YOU'RE AWAKE AT LAST... YOU WERE SLEEPING SO WELL THAT I COULDN'T TELL YOU THAT...
NEVER MIND! COME!
7

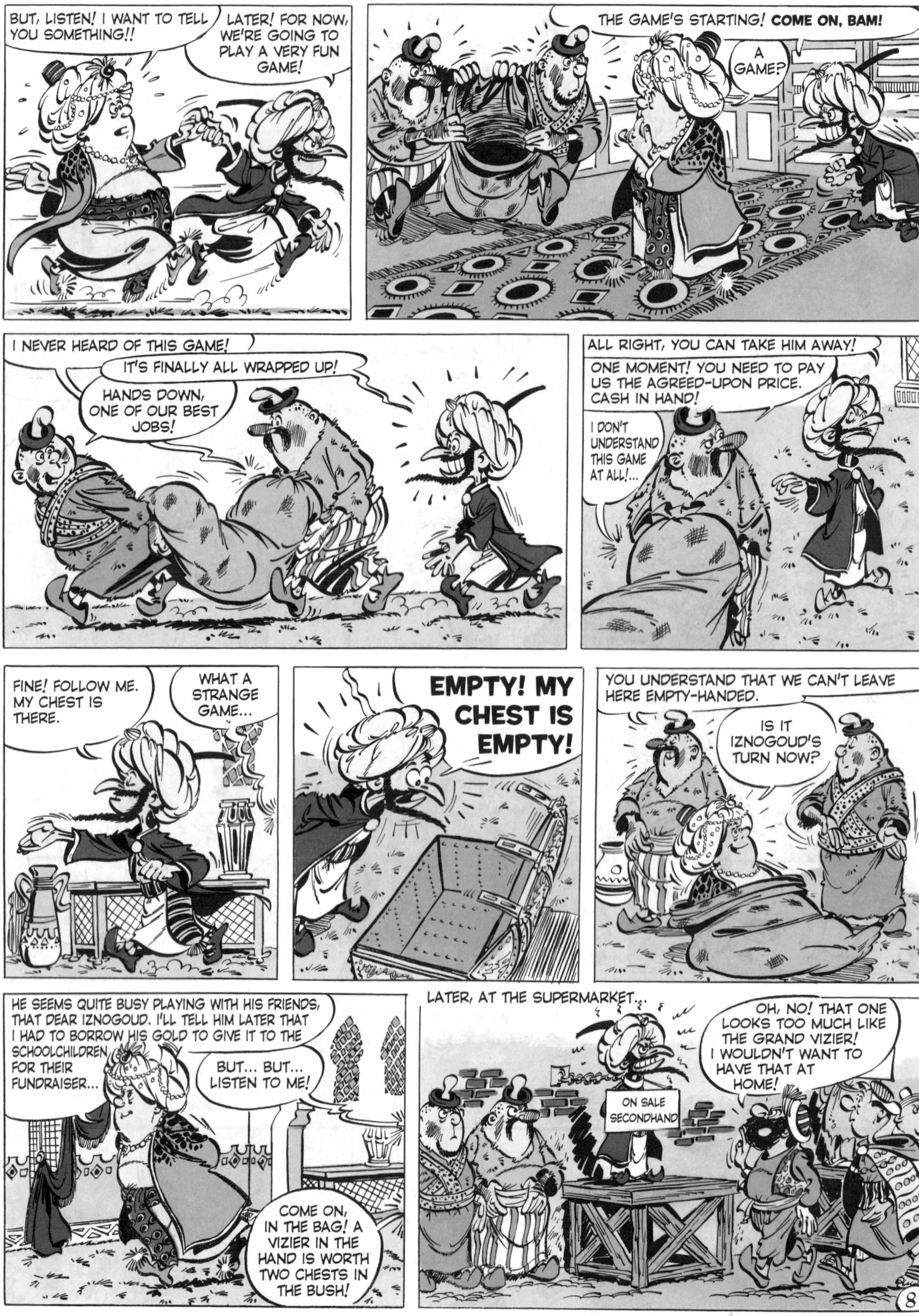
BUT, LISTEN! I WANT TO TELL YOU SOMETHING!!
LATER! FOR NOW, WE'RE GOING TO PLAY A VERY FUN GAME!
THE GAME'S STARTING! COME ON, BAM!
A GAME?
I NEVER HEARD OF THIS GAME!
IT'S FINALLY ALL WRAPPED UP!
HANDS DOWN, ONE OF OUR BEST JOBS!
ALL RIGHT, YOU CAN TAKE HIM AWAY!
ONE MOMENT! YOU NEED TO PAY US THE AGREED-UPON PRICE. CASH IN HAND!
I DON'T UNDERSTAND THIS GAME AT ALL!...
FINE! FOLLOW ME. MY CHEST IS THERE.
WHAT A STRANGE GAME...
EMPTY! MY CHEST IS EMPTY!
YOU UNDERSTAND THAT WE CAN'T LEAVE HERE EMPTY-HANDED.
IS IT IZNOGOUD'S TURN NOW?
HE SEEMS QUITE BUSY PLAYING WITH HIS FRIENDS, THAT DEAR IZNOGOUD. I'LL TELL HIM LATER THAT I HAD TO BORROW HIS GOLD TO GIVE IT TO THE SCHOOLCHILDREN FOR THEIR FUNDRAISER...
BUT... BUT... LISTEN TO ME!
COME ON, IN THE BAG! A VIZIER IN THE HAND IS WORTH TWO CHESTS IN THE BUSH!
LATER, AT THE SUPERMARKET...
ON SALE SECONDHAND
OH, NO! THAT ONE LOOKS TOO MUCH LIKE THE GRAND VIZIER! I WOULDN'T WANT TO HAVE THAT AT HOME!
8

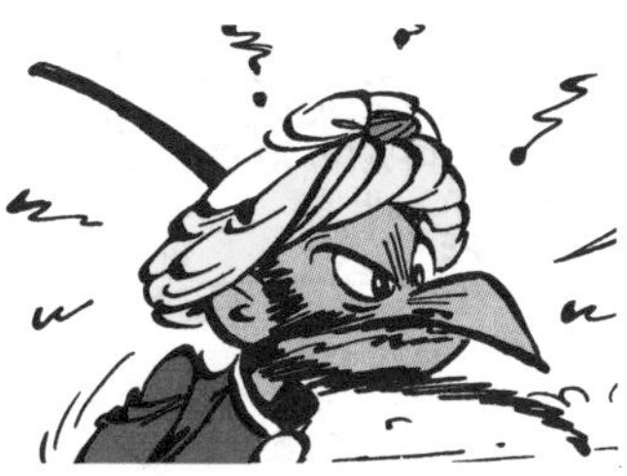

THE HORDE

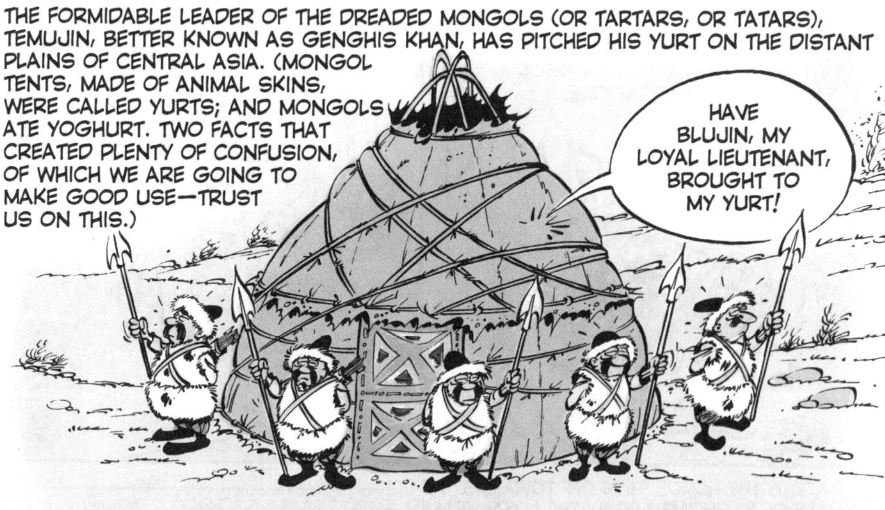
THE FORMIDABLE LEADER OF THE DREADED MONGOLS (OR TARTARS, OR TATARS), TEMUJIN, BETTER KNOWN AS GENGHIS KHAN, HAS PITCHED HIS YURT ON THE DISTANT PLAINS OF CENTRAL ASIA. (MONGOL TENTS, MADE OF ANIMAL SKINS, WERE CALLED YURTS; AND MONGOLS ATE YOGHURT. TWO FACTS THAT CREATED PLENTY OF CONFUSION, OF WHICH WE ARE GOING TO MAKE GOOD USE—TRUST US ON THIS.)
HAVE BLUJIN, MY LOYAL LIEUTENANT, BROUGHT TO MY YURT!

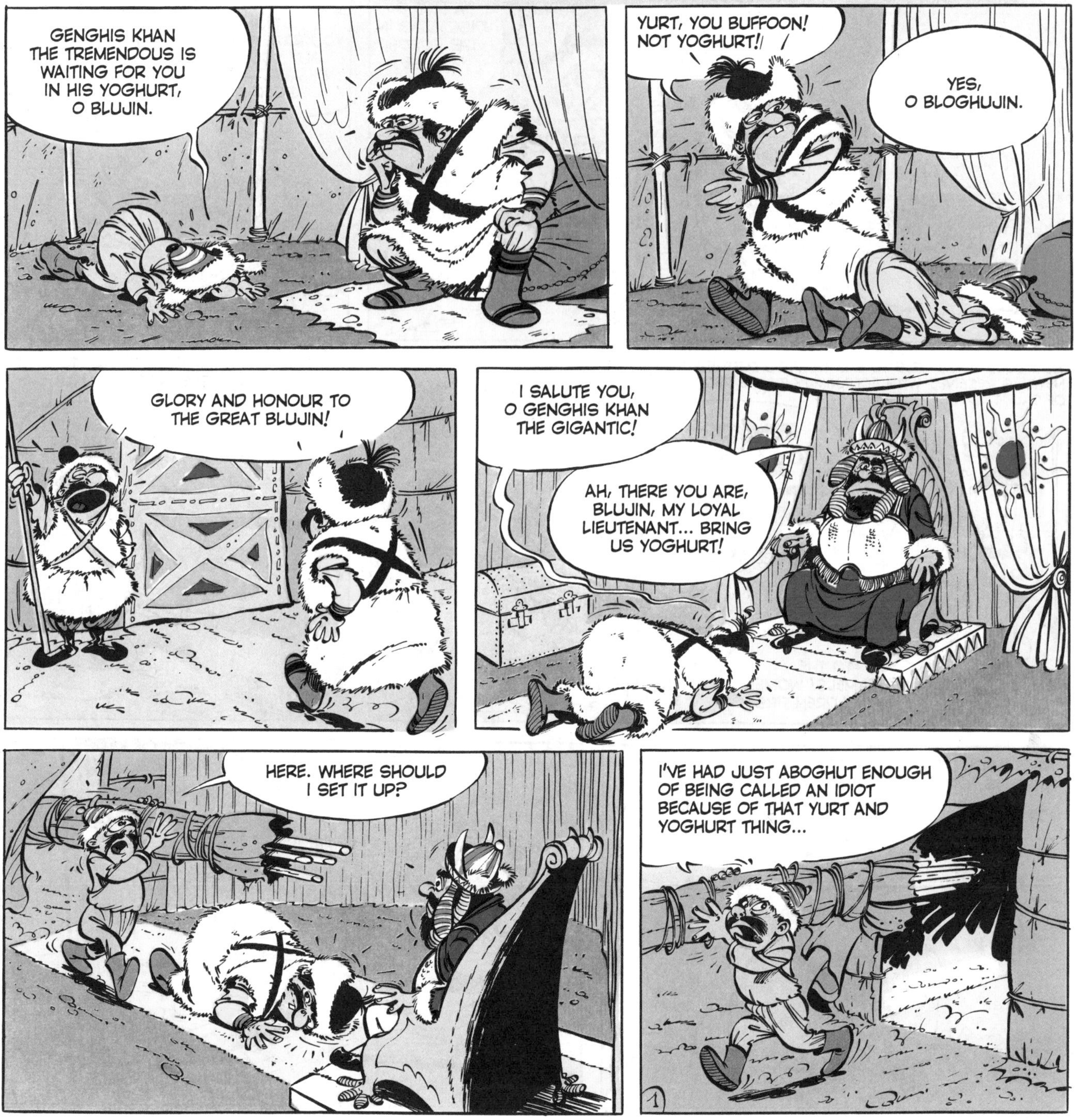
GENGHIS KHAN THE TREMENDOUS IS WAITING FOR YOU IN HIS YOGHURT, O BLUJIN.
YURT, YOU BUFFOON! NOT YOGHURT!
YES, O BLOGHUJIN.
GLORY AND HONOUR TO THE GREAT BLUJIN!
I SALUTE YOU, O GENGHIS KHAN THE GIGANTIC!
AH, THERE YOU ARE, BLUJIN, MY LOYAL LIEUTENANT... BRING US YOGHURT!
HERE. WHERE SHOULD I SET IT UP?
I'VE HAD JUST ABOGHUT ENOUGH OF BEING CALLED AN IDIOT BECAUSE OF THAT YURT AND YOGHURT THING...
1

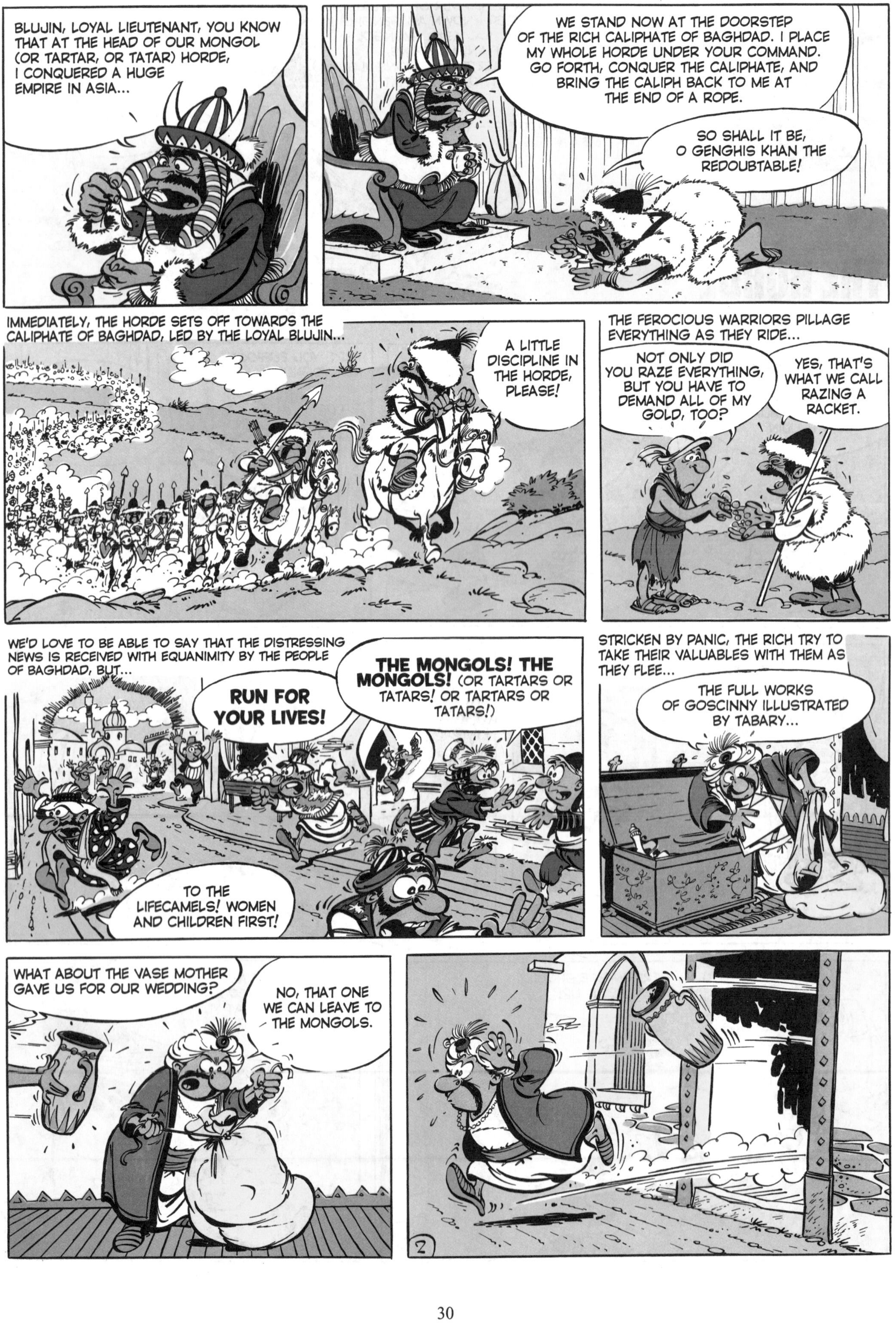
BLUJIN, LOYAL LIEUTENANT, YOU KNOW THAT AT THE HEAD OF OUR MONGOL (OR TARTAR, OR TATAR) HORDE, I CONQUERED A HUGE EMPIRE IN ASIA...
WE STAND NOW AT THE DOORSTEP OF THE RICH CALIPHATE OF BAGHDAD. I PLACE MY WHOLE HORDE UNDER YOUR COMMAND. GO FORTH, CONQUER THE CALIPHATE, AND BRING THE CALIPH BACK TO ME AT THE END OF A ROPE.
SO SHALL IT BE, O GENGHIS KHAN THE REDOUBTABLE!
IMMEDIATELY, THE HORDE SETS OFF TOWARDS THE CALIPHATE OF BAGHDAD, LED BY THE LOYAL BLUJIN...
A LITTLE DISCIPLINE IN THE HORDE, PLEASE!
THE FEROCIOUS WARRIORS PILLAGE EVERYTHING AS THEY RIDE...
NOT ONLY DID YOU RAZE EVERYTHING, BUT YOU HAVE TO DEMAND ALL OF MY GOLD, TOO?
YES, THAT'S WHAT WE CALL RAZING A RACKET.
WE'D LOVE TO BE ABLE TO SAY THAT THE DISTRESSING NEWS IS RECEIVED WITH EQUANIMITY BY THE PEOPLE OF BAGHDAD, BUT...
RUN FOR YOUR LIVES!
THE MONGOLS! THE MONGOLS! (OR TARTARS OR TATARS! OR TARTARS OR TATARS!)
TO THE LIFECAMELS! WOMEN AND CHILDREN FIRST!
STRICKEN BY PANIC, THE RICH TRY TO TAKE THEIR VALUABLES WITH THEM AS THEY FLEE...
THE FULL WORKS OF GOSCINNY ILLUSTRATED BY TABARY...
WHAT ABOUT THE VASE MOTHER GAVE US FOR OUR WEDDING?
NO, THAT ONE WE CAN LEAVE TO THE MONGOLS.

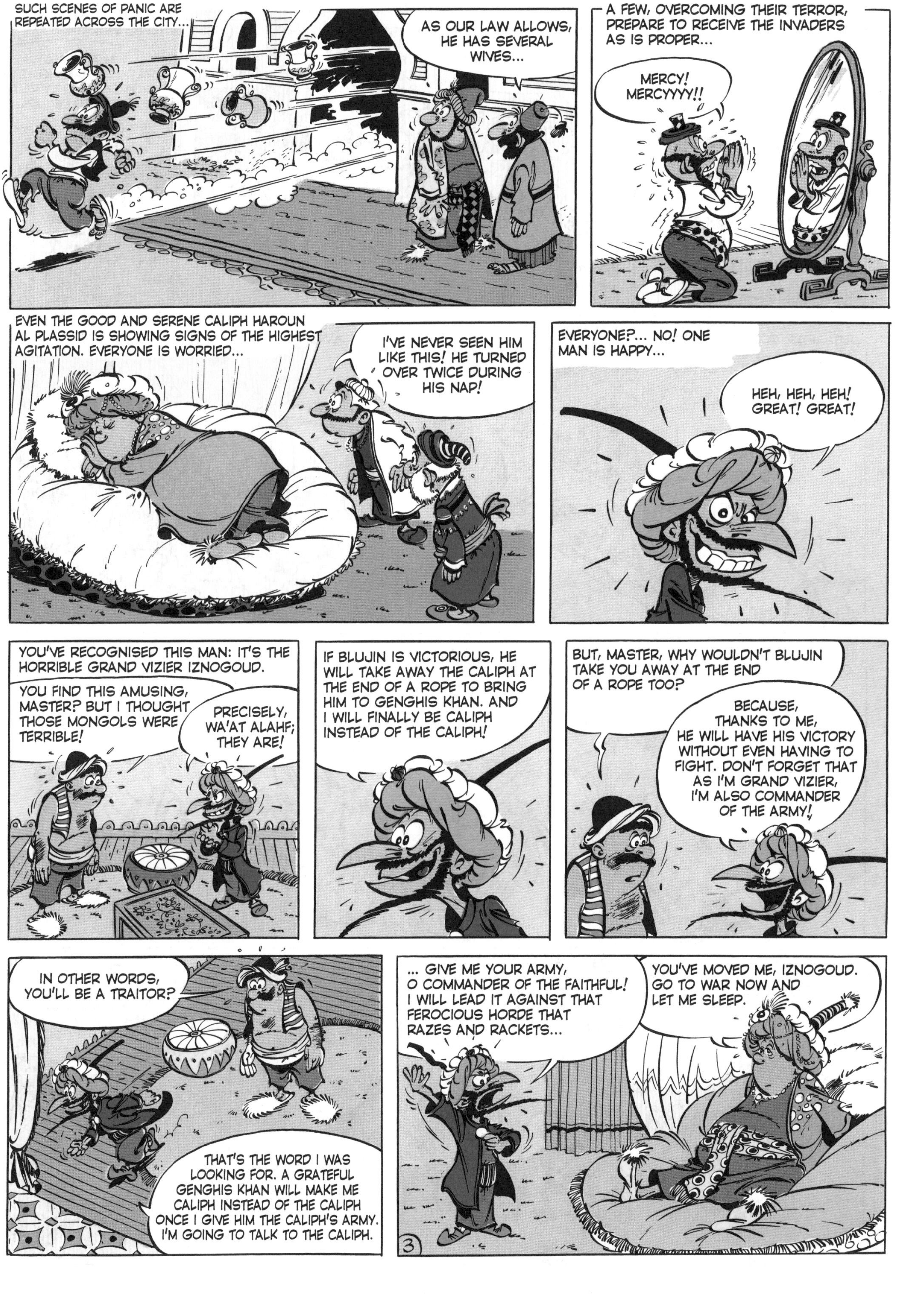
SUCH SCENES OF PANIC ARE REPEATED ACROSS THE CITY...
AS OUR LAW ALLOWS, HE HAS SEVERAL WIVES...
A FEW, OVERCOMING THEIR TERROR, PREPARE TO RECEIVE THE INVADERS AS IS PROPER...
MERCY! MERCYYYY!!
EVEN THE GOOD AND SERENE CALIPH HAROUN AL PLASSID IS SHOWING SIGNS OF THE HIGHEST AGITATION. EVERYONE IS WORRIED...
I'VE NEVER SEEN HIM LIKE THIS! HE TURNED OVER TWICE DURING HIS NAP!
EVERYONE?... NO! ONE MAN IS HAPPY...
HEH, HEH, HEH! GREAT! GREAT!
YOU'VE RECOGNISED THIS MAN: IT'S THE HORRIBLE GRAND VIZIER IZNOGOUD.
YOU FIND THIS AMUSING, MASTER? BUT I THOUGHT THOSE MONGOLS WERE TERRIBLE!
PRECISELY, WA'AT ALAHF; THEY ARE!
IF BLUJIN IS VICTORIOUS, HE WILL TAKE AWAY THE CALIPH AT THE END OF A ROPE TO BRING HIM TO GENGHIS KHAN. AND I WILL FINALLY BE CALIPH INSTEAD OF THE CALIPH!
BUT, MASTER, WHY WOULDN'T BLUJIN TAKE YOU AWAY AT THE END OF A ROPE TOO?
BECAUSE, THANKS TO ME, HE WILL HAVE HIS VICTORY WITHOUT EVEN HAVING TO FIGHT. DON'T FORGET THAT AS I'M GRAND VIZIER, I'M ALSO COMMANDER OF THE ARMY!
IN OTHER WORDS, YOU'LL BE A TRAITOR?
THAT'S THE WORD I WAS LOOKING FOR. A GRATEFUL GENGHIS KHAN WILL MAKE ME CALIPH INSTEAD OF THE CALIPH ONCE I GIVE HIM THE CALIPH'S ARMY. I'M GOING TO TALK TO THE CALIPH.
... GIVE ME YOUR ARMY, O COMMANDER OF THE FAITHFUL! I WILL LEAD IT AGAINST THAT FEROCIOUS HORDE THAT RAZES AND RACKETS...
YOU'VE MOVED ME, IZNOGOUD. GO TO WAR NOW AND LET ME SLEEP.
3

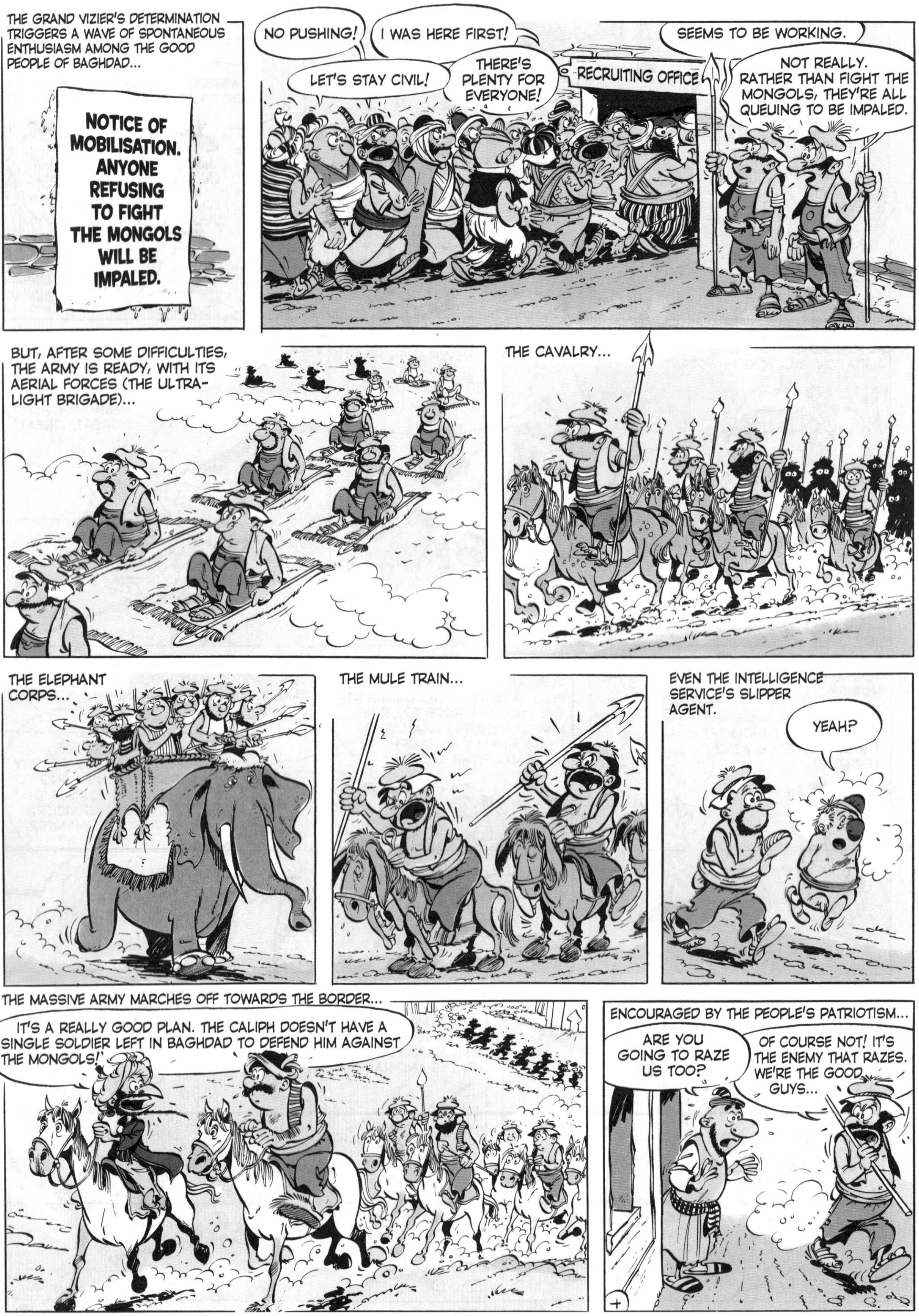
THE GRAND VIZIER'S DETERMINATION TRIGGERS A WAVE OF SPONTANEOUS ENTHUSIASM AMONG THE GOOD PEOPLE OF BAGHDAD...
NOTICE OF MOBILISATION. ANYONE REFUSING TO FIGHT THE MONGOLS WILL BE IMPALED.
NO PUSHING!
I WAS HERE FIRST!
LET'S STAY CIVIL!
THERE'S PLENTY FOR EVERYONE!
RECRUITING OFFICE
SEEMS TO BE WORKING.
NOT REALLY. RATHER THAN FIGHT THE MONGOLS, THEY'RE ALL QUEUING TO BE IMPALED.
BUT, AFTER SOME DIFFICULTIES, THE ARMY IS READY, WITH ITS AERIAL FORCES (THE ULTRA-LIGHT BRIGADE)...
THE CAVALRY...
THE ELEPHANT CORPS...
THE MULE TRAIN...
EVEN THE INTELLIGENCE SERVICE'S SLIPPER AGENT.
YEAH?
THE MASSIVE ARMY MARCHES OFF TOWARDS THE BORDER...
IT'S A REALLY GOOD PLAN. THE CALIPH DOESN'T HAVE A SINGLE SOLDIER LEFT IN BAGHDAD TO DEFEND HIM AGAINST THE MONGOLS!
ENCOURAGED BY THE PEOPLE'S PATRIOTISM...
ARE YOU GOING TO RAZE US TOO?
OF COURSE NOT! IT'S THE ENEMY THAT RAZES. WE'RE THE GOOD GUYS...

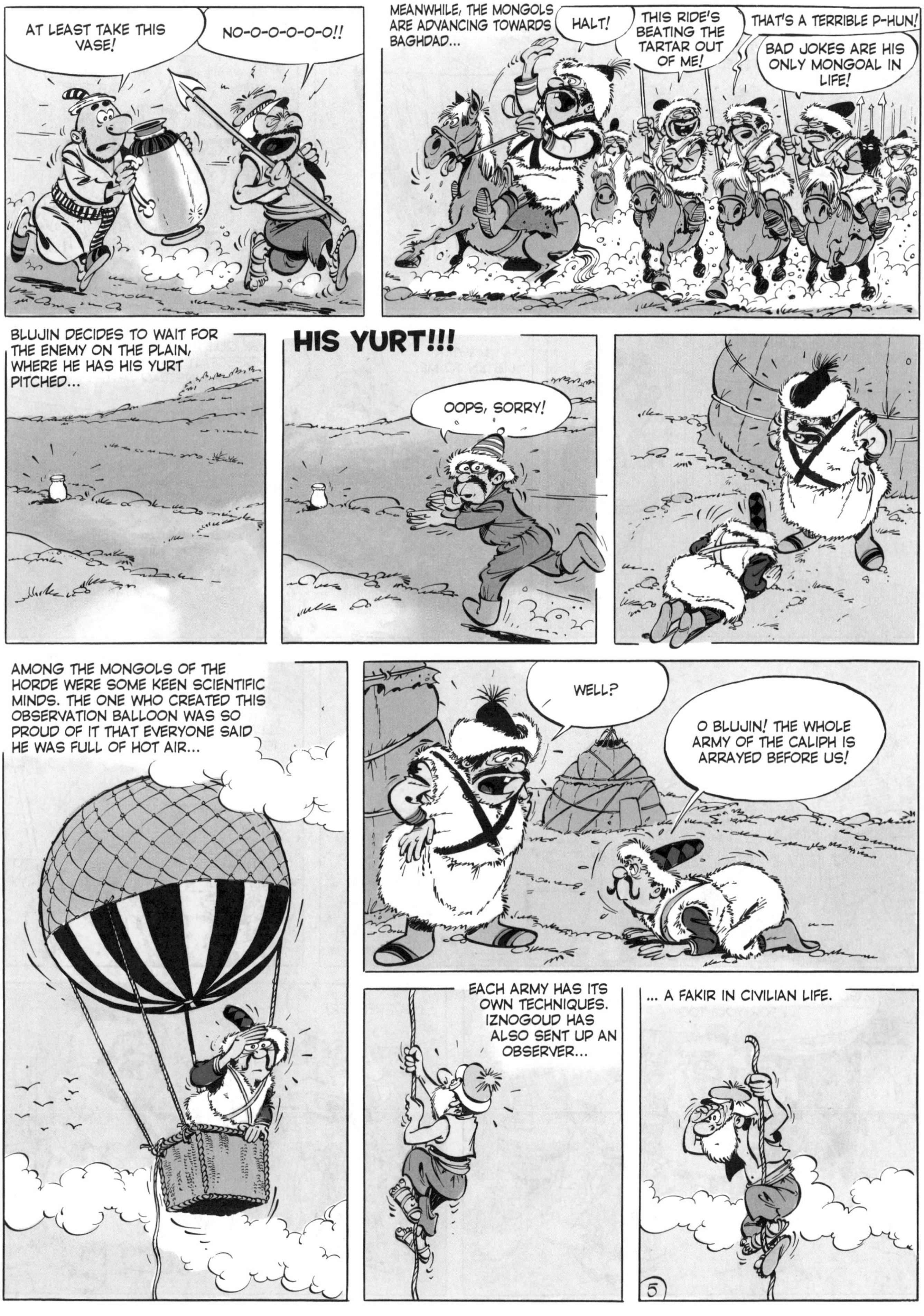
AT LEAST TAKE THIS VASE!
NO-O-O-O-O-O-O!!
MEANWHILE, THE MONGOLS ARE ADVANCING TOWARDS BAGHDAD...
HALT!
THIS RIDE'S BEATING THE TARTAR OUT OF ME!
THAT'S A TERRIBLE P-HUN!
BAD JOKES ARE HIS ONLY MONGOAL IN LIFE!
BLUJIN DECIDES TO WAIT FOR THE ENEMY ON THE PLAIN, WHERE HE HAS HIS YURT PITCHED...
HIS YURT!!!
OOPS, SORRY!
AMONG THE MONGOLS OF THE HORDE WERE SOME KEEN SCIENTIFIC MINDS. THE ONE WHO CREATED THIS OBSERVATION BALLOON WAS SO PROUD OF IT THAT EVERYONE SAID HE WAS FULL OF HOT AIR...
WELL?
O BLUJIN! THE WHOLE ARMY OF THE CALIPH IS ARRAYED BEFORE US!
EACH ARMY HAS ITS OWN TECHNIQUES. IZNOGOUD HAS ALSO SENT UP AN OBSERVER...
... A FAKIR IN CIVILIAN LIFE.
5

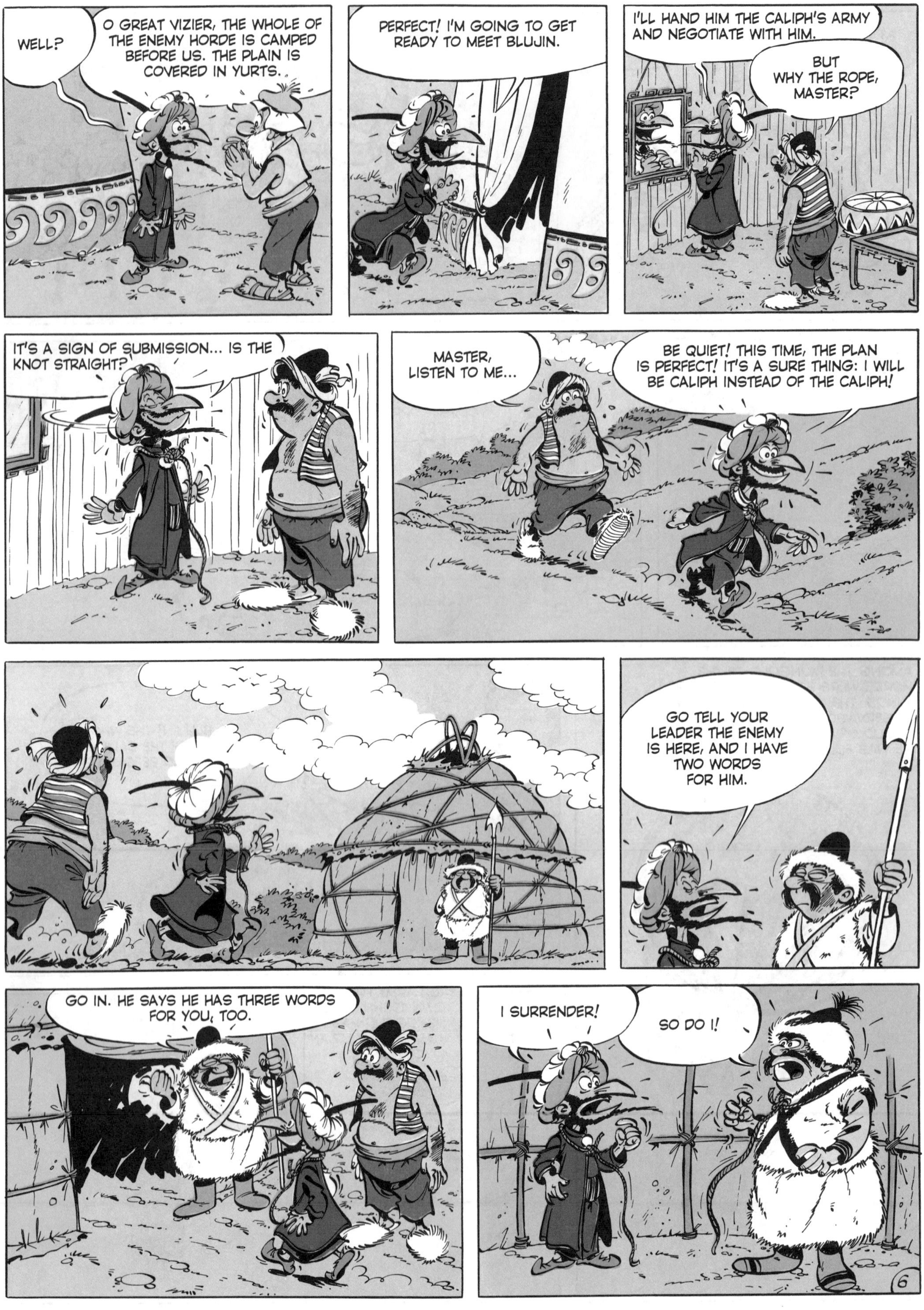

WELL?
O GREAT VIZIER, THE WHOLE OF THE ENEMY HORDE IS CAMPED BEFORE US. THE PLAIN IS COVERED IN YURTS.
PERFECT! I'M GOING TO GET READY TO MEET BLUJIN.
I'LL HAND HIM THE CALIPH'S ARMY AND NEGOTIATE WITH HIM.
BUT WHY THE ROPE, MASTER?
IT'S A SIGN OF SUBMISSION... IS THE KNOT STRAIGHT?
MASTER, LISTEN TO ME...
BE QUIET! THIS TIME, THE PLAN IS PERFECT! IT'S A SURE THING: I WILL BE CALIPH INSTEAD OF THE CALIPH!
GO TELL YOUR LEADER THE ENEMY IS HERE, AND I HAVE TWO WORDS FOR HIM.
GO IN. HE SAYS HE HAS THREE WORDS FOR YOU, TOO.
I SURRENDER!
SO DO I!
6

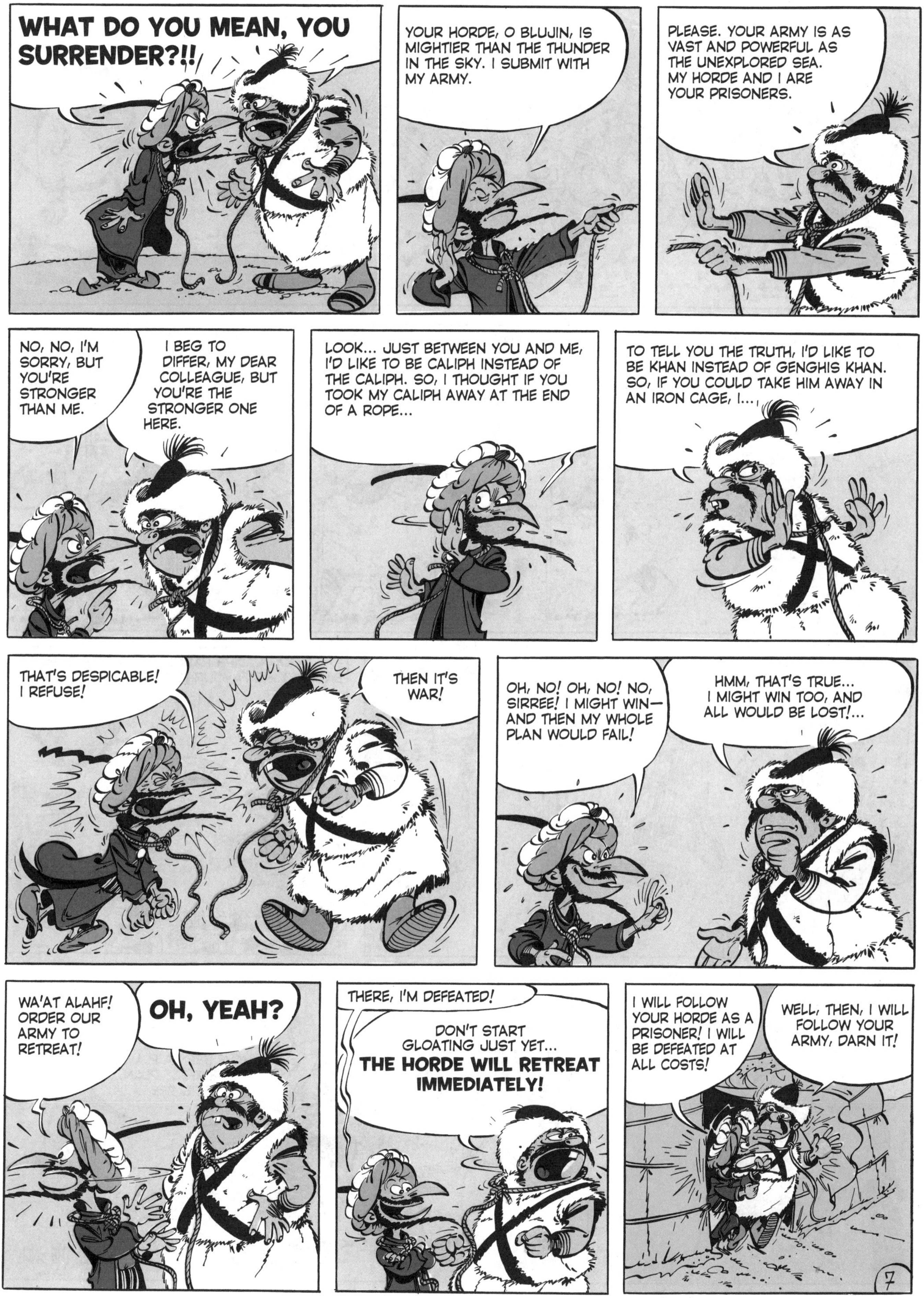
WHAT DO YOU MEAN, YOU SURRENDER?!!
YOUR HORDE, O BLUJIN, IS MIGHTIER THAN THE THUNDER IN THE SKY. I SUBMIT WITH MY ARMY.
PLEASE. YOUR ARMY IS AS VAST AND POWERFUL AS THE UNEXPLORED SEA. MY HORDE AND I ARE YOUR PRISONERS.
NO, NO, I'M SORRY, BUT YOU'RE STRONGER THAN ME.
I BEG TO DIFFER, MY DEAR COLLEAGUE, BUT YOU'RE THE STRONGER ONE HERE.
LOOK... JUST BETWEEN YOU AND ME, I'D LIKE TO BE CALIPH INSTEAD OF THE CALIPH. SO, I THOUGHT IF YOU TOOK MY CALIPH AWAY AT THE END OF A ROPE...
TO TELL YOU THE TRUTH, I'D LIKE TO BE KHAN INSTEAD OF GENGHIS KHAN. SO, IF YOU COULD TAKE HIM AWAY IN AN IRON CAGE, I...
THAT'S DESPICABLE! I REFUSE!
THEN IT'S WAR!
OH, NO! OH, NO! NO, SIRREE! I MIGHT WIN— AND THEN MY WHOLE PLAN WOULD FAIL!
HMM, THAT'S TRUE... I MIGHT WIN TOO, AND ALL WOULD BE LOST!...
WA'AT ALAHF! ORDER OUR ARMY TO RETREAT!
OH, YEAH?
THERE, I'M DEFEATED!
DON'T START GLOATING JUST YET... THE HORDE WILL RETREAT IMMEDIATELY!
I WILL FOLLOW YOUR HORDE AS A PRISONER! I WILL BE DEFEATED AT ALL COSTS!
WELL, THEN, I WILL FOLLOW YOUR ARMY, DARN IT!
7

AND SO, THE CALIPH'S ARMY RETREATS, BRINGING ALONG ONE PRISONER...

HURRY UP, BOYS! THERE'S A MONGOL PURSUING US!

WHILE THE MONGOL HORDE FALLS BACK, TAKING THEIR OWN PRISONER.

SHEESH, WHAT A CLINGY FELLOW!... WHAT DOES HE WANT WITH US, ANYWAY?

AND SO IT IS THAT THE WAR ENDS, WITH A DOUBLE DEFEAT, TO THE QUASI-GENERAL SATISFACTION OF THE PEOPLE OF BAGHDAD...

THE GOOD CALIPH HAROUN AL PLASSID GOES BACK TO HIS FAVOURITE PASTIMES...

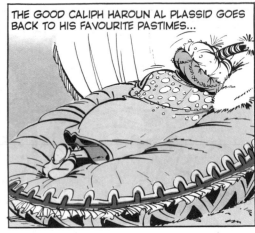

AS FOR GENGHIS KHAN, IMPRESSED...

MY HORDE FELL BACK FOR THE FIRST TIME EVER... THAT'S NOT A GOOD SIGN...

... HE GOES BACK EAST FOR GOOD, WITH HIS YURTS, HIS YOGHURTS AND HIS PRISONER.

LET'S SEE... THERE SEEMS TO HAVE BEEN A FLAW IN MY PERFECT PLAN... LET'S SEE...

THE END

A LOOKALIKE

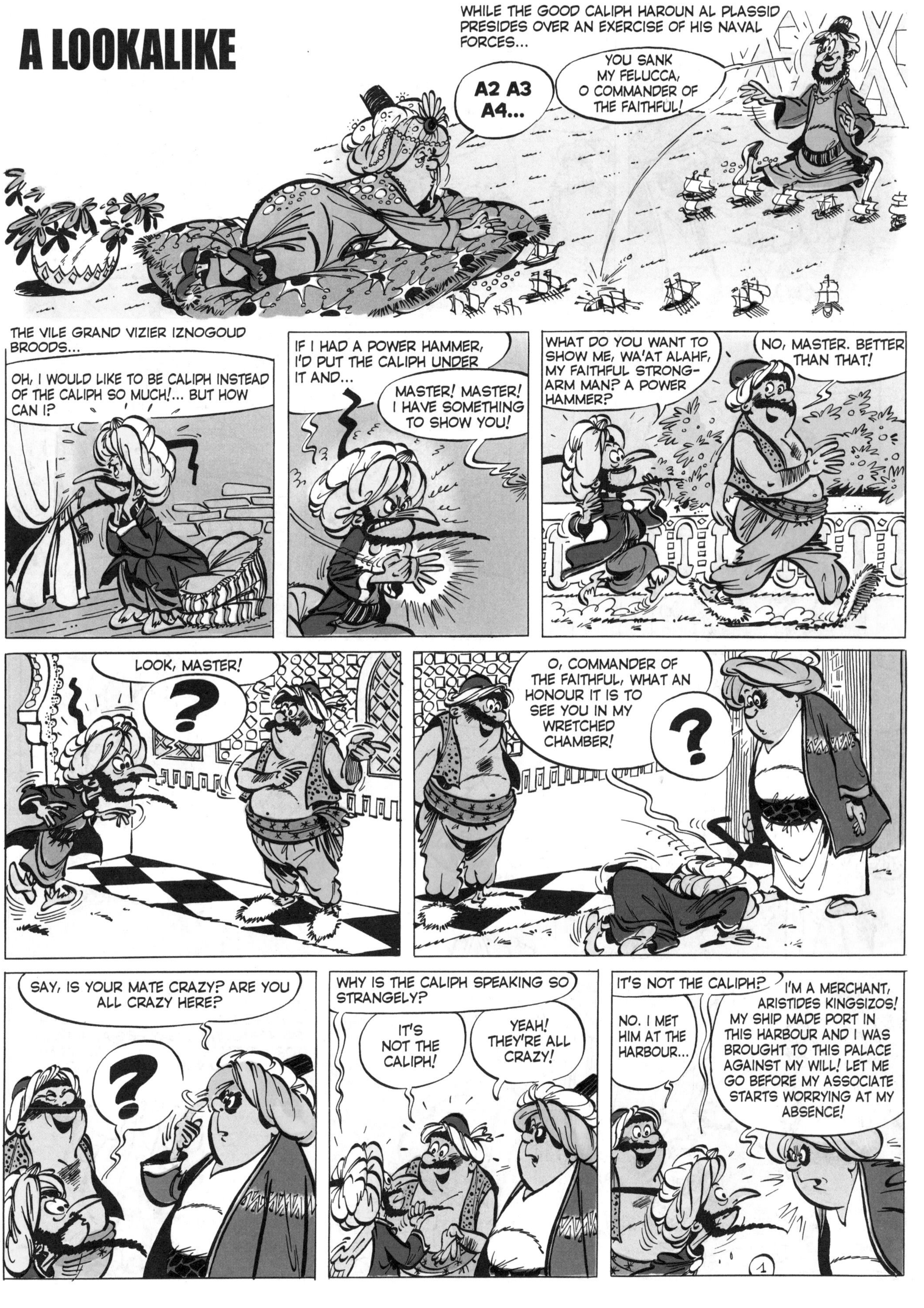
WHILE THE GOOD CALIPH HAROUN AL PLASSID PRESIDES OVER AN EXERCISE OF HIS NAVAL FORCES...
YOU SANK MY FELUCCA, O COMMANDER OF THE FAITHFUL!
A2 A3 A4...
THE VILE GRAND VIZIER IZNOGOUD BROODS...
OH, I WOULD LIKE TO BE CALIPH INSTEAD OF THE CALIPH SO MUCH!... BUT HOW CAN I?
IF I HAD A POWER HAMMER, I'D PUT THE CALIPH UNDER IT AND...
MASTER! MASTER! I HAVE SOMETHING TO SHOW YOU!
WHAT DO YOU WANT TO SHOW ME, WA'AT ALAHF, MY FAITHFUL STRONG-ARM MAN? A POWER HAMMER?
NO, MASTER. BETTER THAN THAT!
LOOK, MASTER!
?
O, COMMANDER OF THE FAITHFUL, WHAT AN HONOUR IT IS TO SEE YOU IN MY WRETCHED CHAMBER!
?
SAY, IS YOUR MATE CRAZY? ARE YOU ALL CRAZY HERE?
?
WHY IS THE CALIPH SPEAKING SO STRANGELY?
IT'S NOT THE CALIPH!
YEAH! THEY'RE ALL CRAZY!
IT'S NOT THE CALIPH?
NO. I MET HIM AT THE HARBOUR...
I'M A MERCHANT, ARISTIDES KINGSIZOS! MY SHIP MADE PORT IN THIS HARBOUR AND I WAS BROUGHT TO THIS PALACE AGAINST MY WILL! LET ME GO BEFORE MY ASSOCIATE STARTS WORRYING AT MY ABSENCE!
1

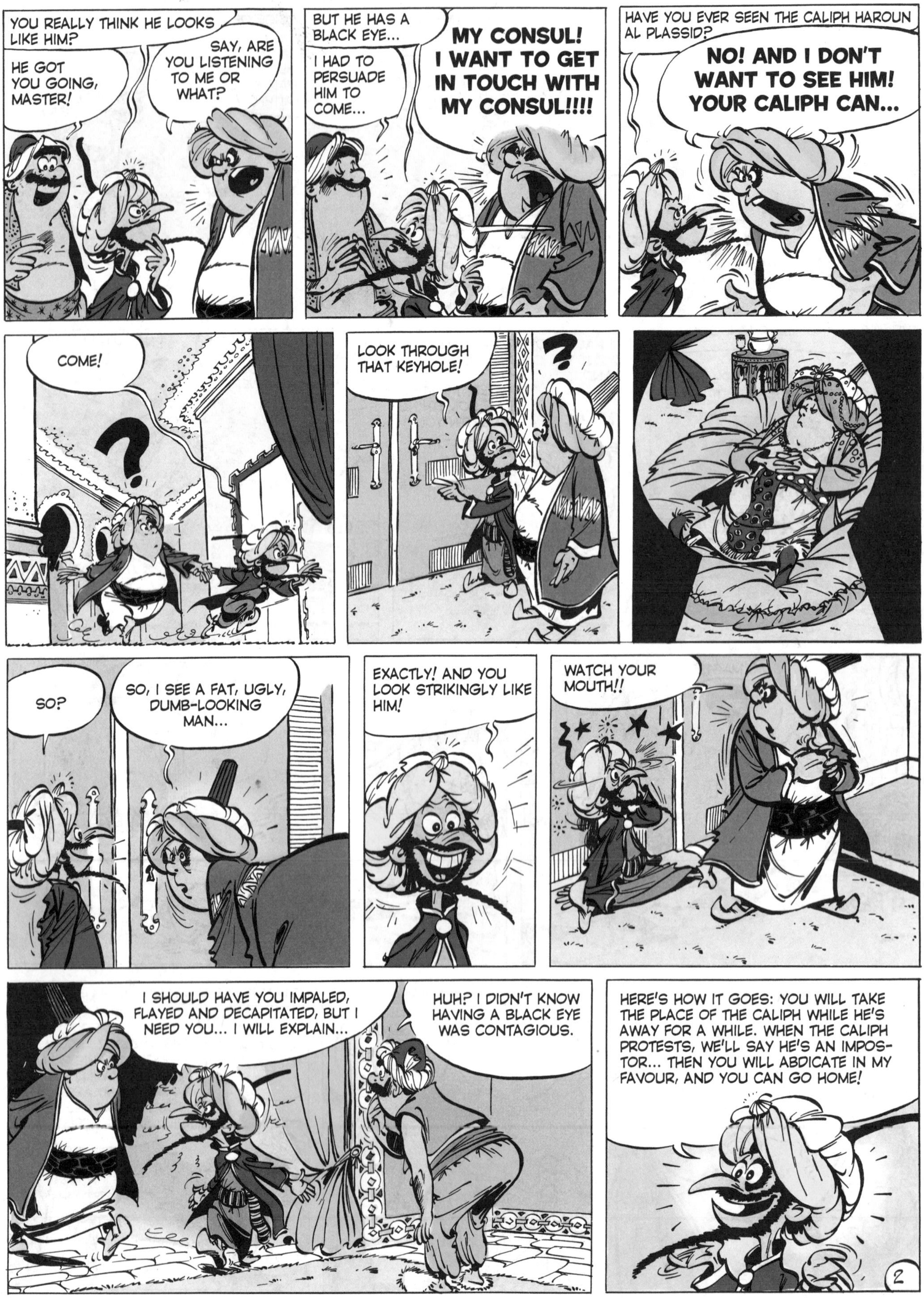
YOU REALLY THINK HE LOOKS LIKE HIM?
HE GOT YOU GOING, MASTER!
SAY, ARE YOU LISTENING TO ME OR WHAT?
BUT HE HAS A BLACK EYE...
I HAD TO PERSUADE HIM TO COME...
MY CONSUL! I WANT TO GET IN TOUCH WITH MY CONSUL!!!!
HAVE YOU EVER SEEN THE CALIPH HAROUN AL PLASSID?
NO! AND I DON'T WANT TO SEE HIM! YOUR CALIPH CAN...
COME!
LOOK THROUGH THAT KEYHOLE!
SO?
SO, I SEE A FAT, UGLY, DUMB-LOOKING MAN...
EXACTLY! AND YOU LOOK STRIKINGLY LIKE HIM!
WATCH YOUR MOUTH!!
I SHOULD HAVE YOU IMPALED, FLAYED AND DECAPITATED, BUT I NEED YOU... I WILL EXPLAIN...
HUH? I DIDN'T KNOW HAVING A BLACK EYE WAS CONTAGIOUS.
HERE'S HOW IT GOES: YOU WILL TAKE THE PLACE OF THE CALIPH WHILE HE'S AWAY FOR A WHILE. WHEN THE CALIPH PROTESTS, WE'LL SAY HE'S AN IMPOSTOR... THEN YOU WILL ABDICATE IN MY FAVOUR, AND YOU CAN GO HOME!
2

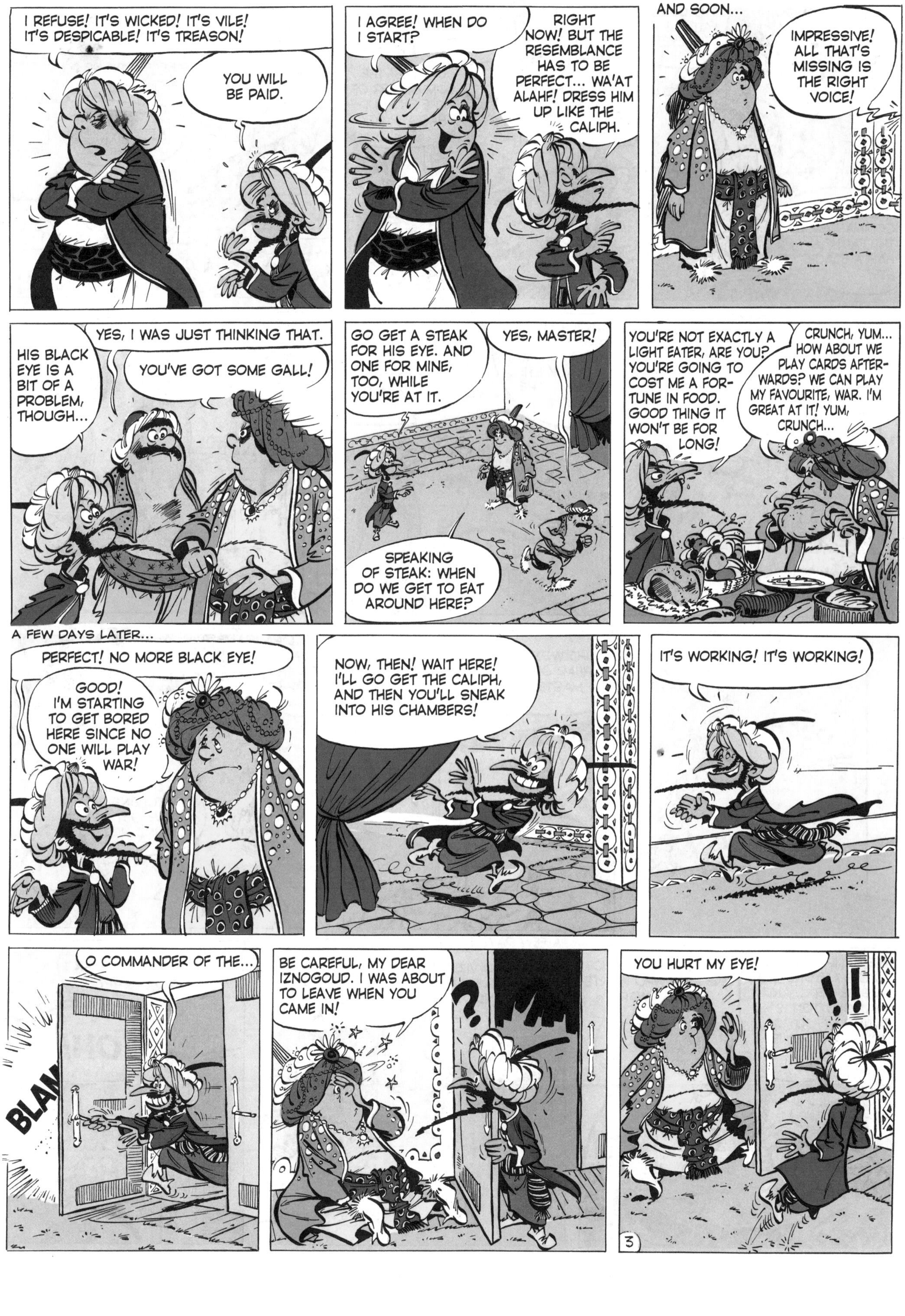
I REFUSE! IT'S WICKED! IT'S VILE! IT'S DESPICABLE! IT'S TREASON!
YOU WILL BE PAID.
I AGREE! WHEN DO I START?
RIGHT NOW! BUT THE RESEMBLANCE HAS TO BE PERFECT... WA'AT ALAHF! DRESS HIM UP LIKE THE CALIPH.
AND SOON...
IMPRESSIVE! ALL THAT'S MISSING IS THE RIGHT VOICE!
HIS BLACK EYE IS A BIT OF A PROBLEM, THOUGH...
YES, I WAS JUST THINKING THAT.
YOU'VE GOT SOME GALL!
GO GET A STEAK FOR HIS EYE. AND ONE FOR MINE, TOO, WHILE YOU'RE AT IT.
YES, MASTER!
SPEAKING OF STEAK: WHEN DO WE GET TO EAT AROUND HERE?
YOU'RE NOT EXACTLY A LIGHT EATER, ARE YOU? YOU'RE GOING TO COST ME A FORTUNE IN FOOD. GOOD THING IT WON'T BE FOR LONG!
CRUNCH, YUM... HOW ABOUT WE PLAY CARDS AFTERWARDS? WE CAN PLAY MY FAVOURITE, WAR. I'M GREAT AT IT! YUM, CRUNCH...
A FEW DAYS LATER...
PERFECT! NO MORE BLACK EYE!
GOOD! I'M STARTING TO GET BORED HERE SINCE NO ONE WILL PLAY WAR!
NOW, THEN! WAIT HERE! I'LL GO GET THE CALIPH, AND THEN YOU'LL SNEAK INTO HIS CHAMBERS!
IT'S WORKING! IT'S WORKING!
O COMMANDER OF THE...
BLAM
BE CAREFUL, MY DEAR IZNOGOUD. I WAS ABOUT TO LEAVE WHEN YOU CAME IN!
?
YOU HURT MY EYE!
!!
3

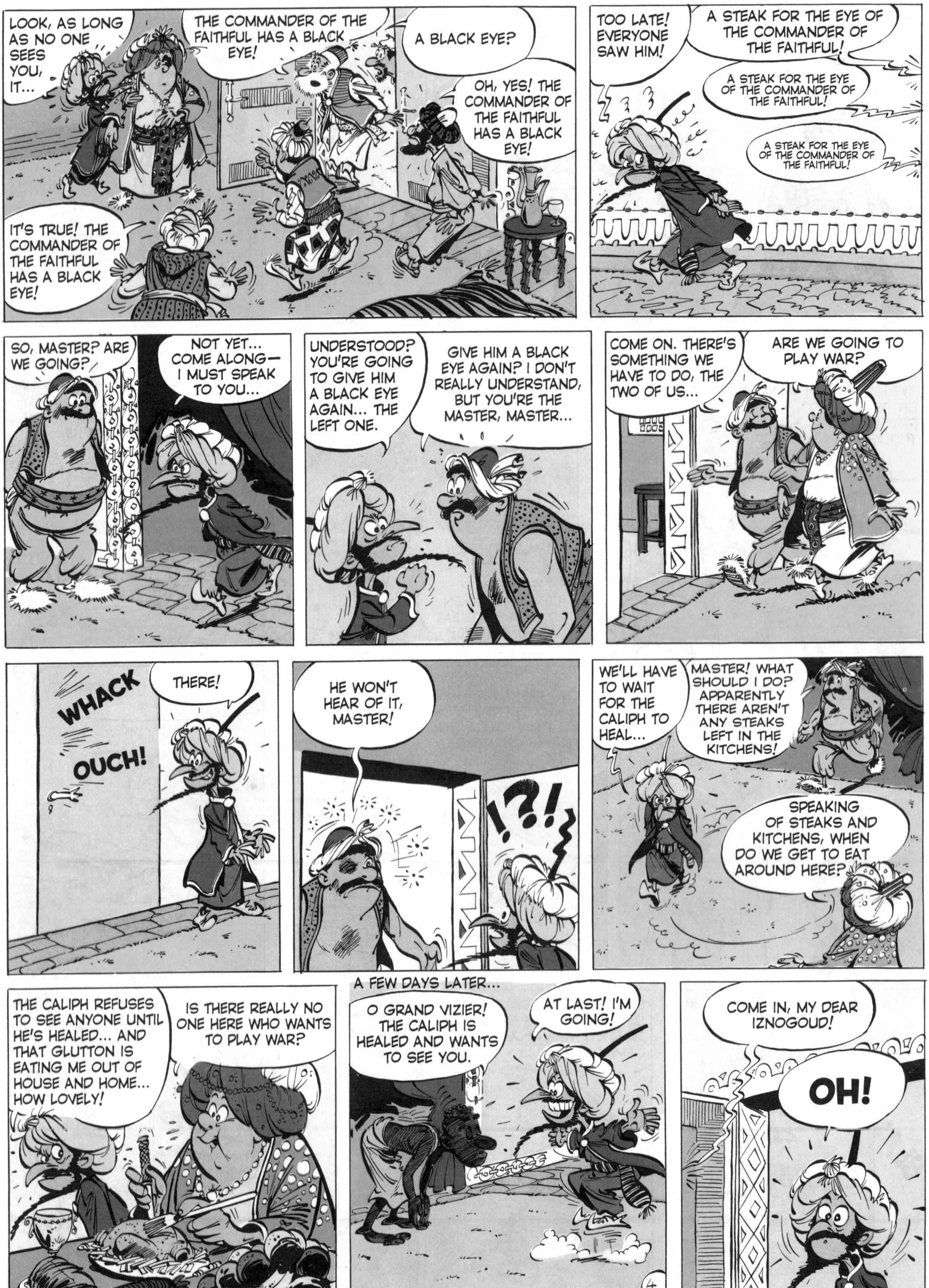
LOOK, AS LONG AS NO ONE SEES YOU, IT...
THE COMMANDER OF THE FAITHFUL HAS A BLACK EYE!
A BLACK EYE?
OH, YES! THE COMMANDER OF THE FAITHFUL HAS A BLACK EYE!
IT'S TRUE! THE COMMANDER OF THE FAITHFUL HAS A BLACK EYE!
TOO LATE! EVERYONE SAW HIM!
A STEAK FOR THE EYE OF THE COMMANDER OF THE FAITHFUL!
A STEAK FOR THE EYE OF THE COMMANDER OF THE FAITHFUL!
A STEAK FOR THE EYE OF THE COMMANDER OF THE FAITHFUL!
SO, MASTER? ARE WE GOING?
NOT YET... COME ALONG— I MUST SPEAK TO YOU...
UNDERSTOOD? YOU'RE GOING TO GIVE HIM A BLACK EYE AGAIN... THE LEFT ONE.
GIVE HIM A BLACK EYE AGAIN? I DON'T REALLY UNDERSTAND, BUT YOU'RE THE MASTER, MASTER...
COME ON. THERE'S SOMETHING WE HAVE TO DO, THE TWO OF US...
ARE WE GOING TO PLAY WAR?
WHACK
OUCH!
THERE!
HE WON'T HEAR OF IT, MASTER!
!?!
WE'LL HAVE TO WAIT FOR THE CALIPH TO HEAL...
MASTER! WHAT SHOULD I DO? APPARENTLY THERE AREN'T ANY STEAKS LEFT IN THE KITCHENS!
SPEAKING OF STEAKS AND KITCHENS, WHEN DO WE GET TO EAT AROUND HERE?
THE CALIPH REFUSES TO SEE ANYONE UNTIL HE'S HEALED... AND THAT GLUTTON IS EATING ME OUT OF HOUSE AND HOME... HOW LOVELY!
IS THERE REALLY NO ONE HERE WHO WANTS TO PLAY WAR?
A FEW DAYS LATER...
O GRAND VIZIER! THE CALIPH IS HEALED AND WANTS TO SEE YOU.
AT LAST! I'M GOING!
4
COME IN, MY DEAR IZNOGOUD!
OH!

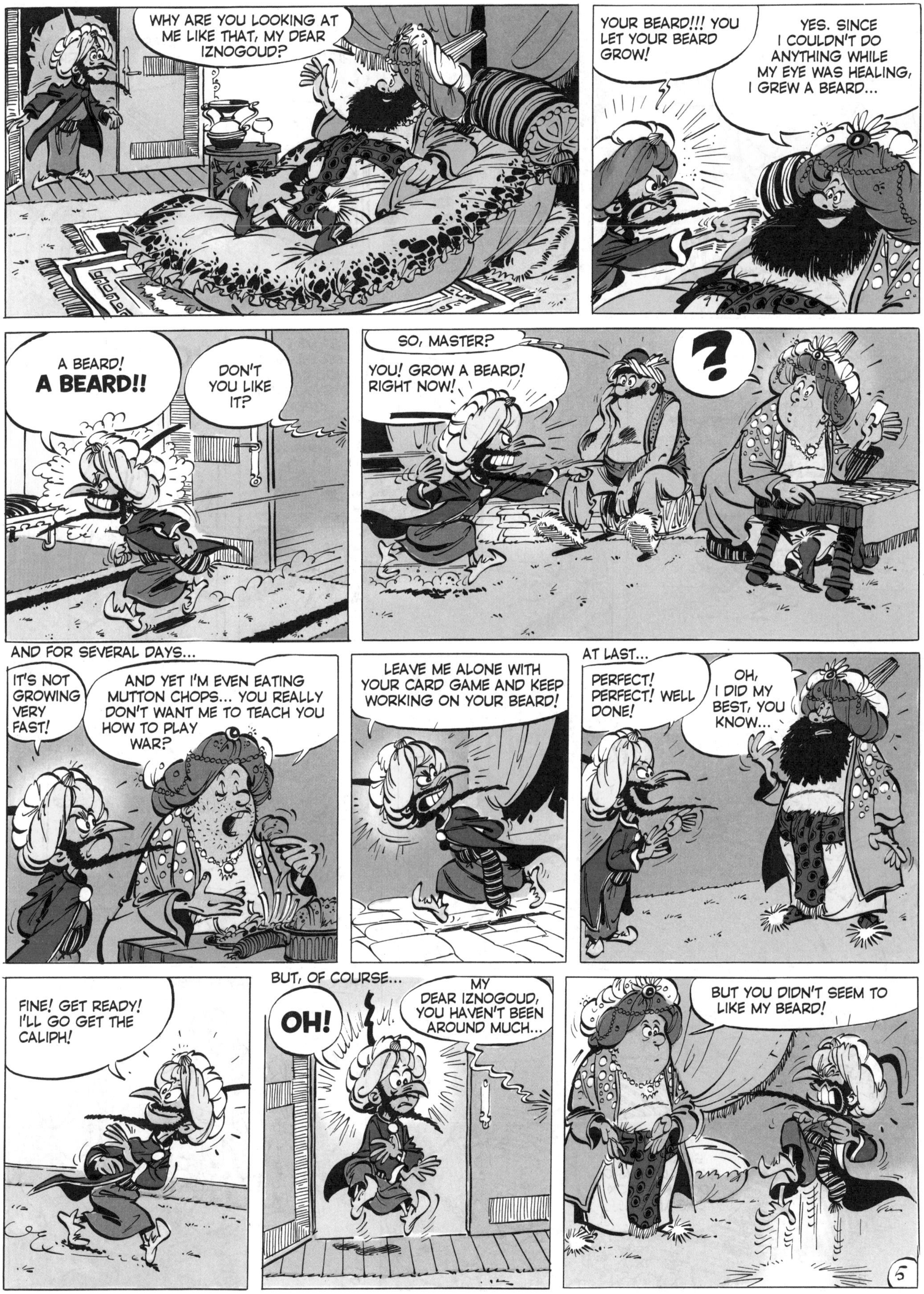
WHY ARE YOU LOOKING AT ME LIKE THAT, MY DEAR IZNOGOUD?
YOUR BEARD!!! YOU LET YOUR BEARD GROW!
YES. SINCE I COULDN'T DO ANYTHING WHILE MY EYE WAS HEALING, I GREW A BEARD...
A BEARD! A BEARD!!
DON'T YOU LIKE IT?
SO, MASTER?
YOU! GROW A BEARD! RIGHT NOW!
?
AND FOR SEVERAL DAYS...
IT'S NOT GROWING VERY FAST!
AND YET I'M EVEN EATING MUTTON CHOPS... YOU REALLY DON'T WANT ME TO TEACH YOU HOW TO PLAY WAR?
LEAVE ME ALONE WITH YOUR CARD GAME AND KEEP WORKING ON YOUR BEARD!
AT LAST...
PERFECT! PERFECT! WELL DONE!
OH, I DID MY BEST, YOU KNOW...
FINE! GET READY! I'LL GO GET THE CALIPH!
BUT, OF COURSE...
OH!
MY DEAR IZNOGOUD, YOU HAVEN'T BEEN AROUND MUCH...
BUT YOU DIDN'T SEEM TO LIKE MY BEARD!
5

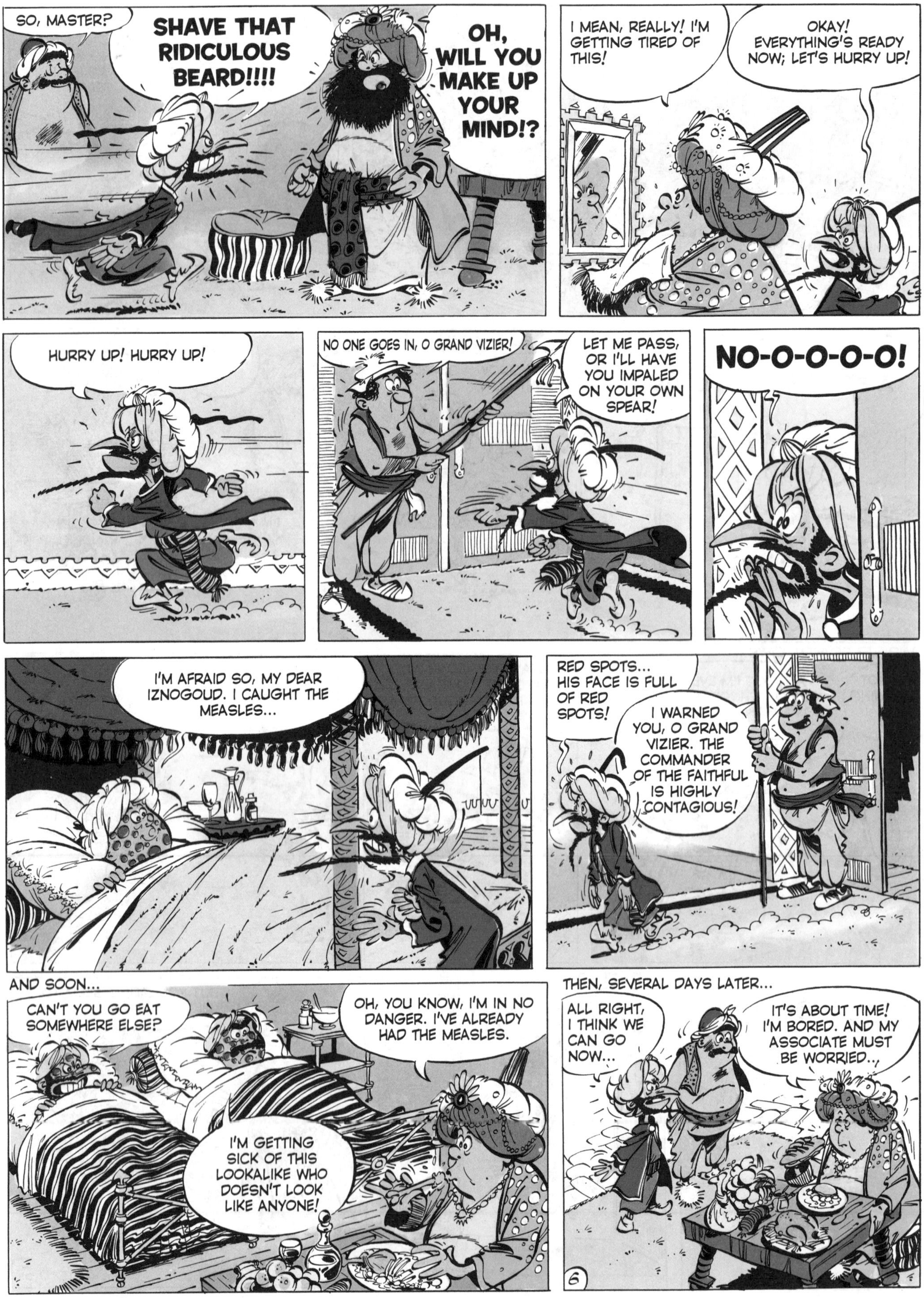
SO, MASTER?
SHAVE THAT RIDICULOUS BEARD!!!!
OH, WILL YOU MAKE UP YOUR MIND!?
I MEAN, REALLY! I'M GETTING TIRED OF THIS!
OKAY! EVERYTHING'S READY NOW; LET'S HURRY UP!
HURRY UP! HURRY UP!
NO ONE GOES IN, O GRAND VIZIER!
LET ME PASS, OR I'LL HAVE YOU IMPALED ON YOUR OWN SPEAR!
NO-O-O-O-O!
I'M AFRAID SO, MY DEAR IZNOGOUD. I CAUGHT THE MEASLES...
RED SPOTS... HIS FACE IS FULL OF RED SPOTS!
I WARNED YOU, O GRAND VIZIER. THE COMMANDER OF THE FAITHFUL IS HIGHLY CONTAGIOUS!
AND SOON...
CAN'T YOU GO EAT SOMEWHERE ELSE?
OH, YOU KNOW, I'M IN NO DANGER. I'VE ALREADY HAD THE MEASLES.
I'M GETTING SICK OF THIS LOOKALIKE WHO DOESN'T LOOK LIKE ANYONE!
THEN, SEVERAL DAYS LATER...
ALL RIGHT, I THINK WE CAN GO NOW...
IT'S ABOUT TIME! I'M BORED. AND MY ASSOCIATE MUST BE WORRIED...
6

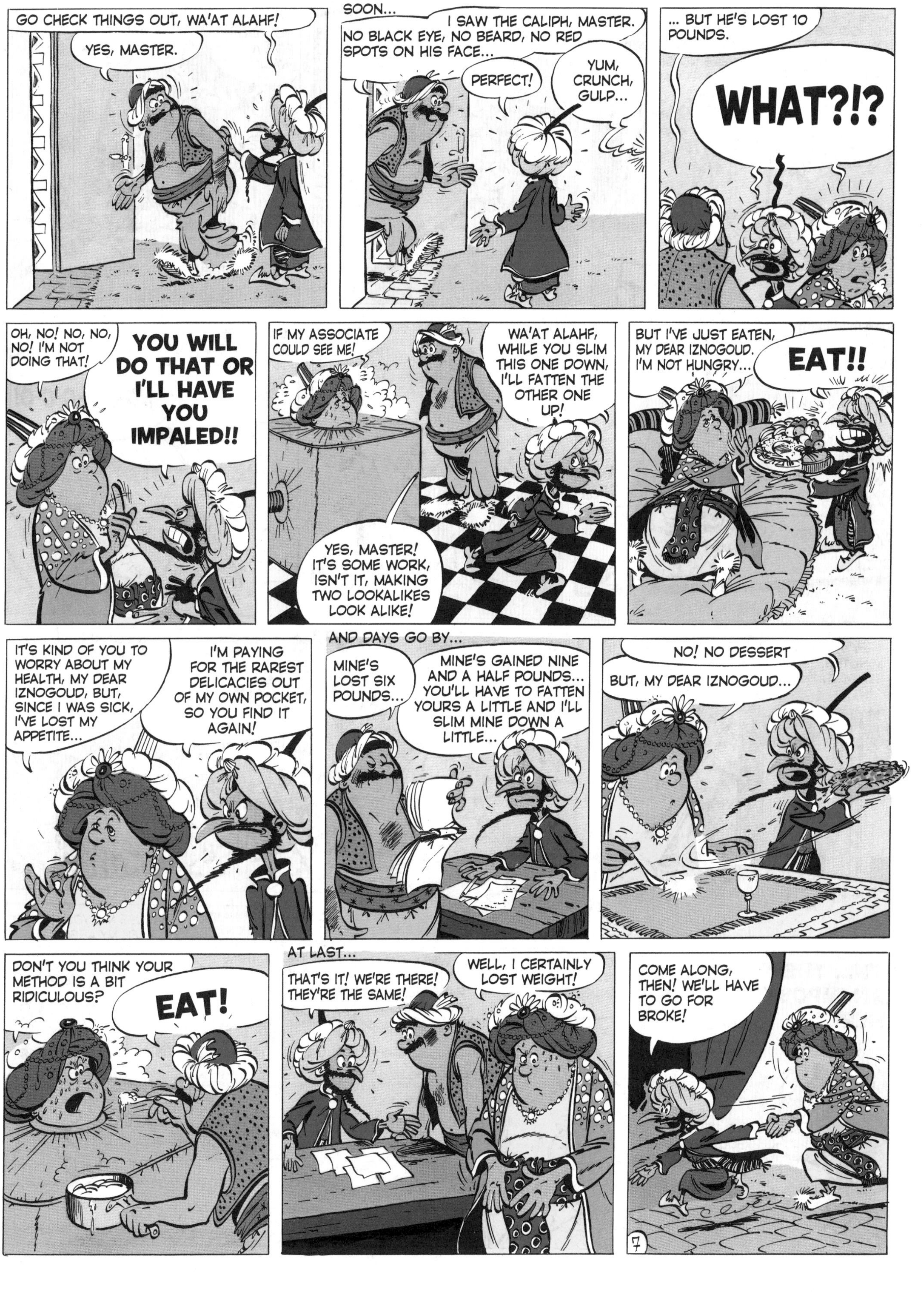
GO CHECK THINGS OUT, WA'AT ALAHF!
YES, MASTER.
SOON...
I SAW THE CALIPH, MASTER. NO BLACK EYE, NO BEARD, NO RED SPOTS ON HIS FACE...
PERFECT!
YUM, CRUNCH, GULP...
... BUT HE'S LOST 10 POUNDS.
WHAT?!?
OH, NO! NO, NO, NO! I'M NOT DOING THAT!
YOU WILL DO THAT OR I'LL HAVE YOU IMPALED!!
IF MY ASSOCIATE COULD SEE ME!
WA'AT ALAHF, WHILE YOU SLIM THIS ONE DOWN, I'LL FATTEN THE OTHER ONE UP!
YES, MASTER! IT'S SOME WORK, ISN'T IT, MAKING TWO LOOKALIKES LOOK ALIKE!
BUT I'VE JUST EATEN, MY DEAR IZNOGOUD. I'M NOT HUNGRY...
EAT!!
IT'S KIND OF YOU TO WORRY ABOUT MY HEALTH, MY DEAR IZNOGOUD, BUT, SINCE I WAS SICK, I'VE LOST MY APPETITE...
I'M PAYING FOR THE RAREST DELICACIES OUT OF MY OWN POCKET, SO YOU FIND IT AGAIN!
AND DAYS GO BY...
MINE'S LOST SIX POUNDS...
MINE'S GAINED NINE AND A HALF POUNDS... YOU'LL HAVE TO FATTEN YOURS A LITTLE AND I'LL SLIM MINE DOWN A LITTLE...
NO! NO DESSERT
BUT, MY DEAR IZNOGOUD...
DON'T YOU THINK YOUR METHOD IS A BIT RIDICULOUS?
EAT!
AT LAST...
THAT'S IT! WE'RE THERE! THEY'RE THE SAME!
WELL, I CERTAINLY LOST WEIGHT!
COME ALONG, THEN! WE'LL HAVE TO GO FOR BROKE!
7

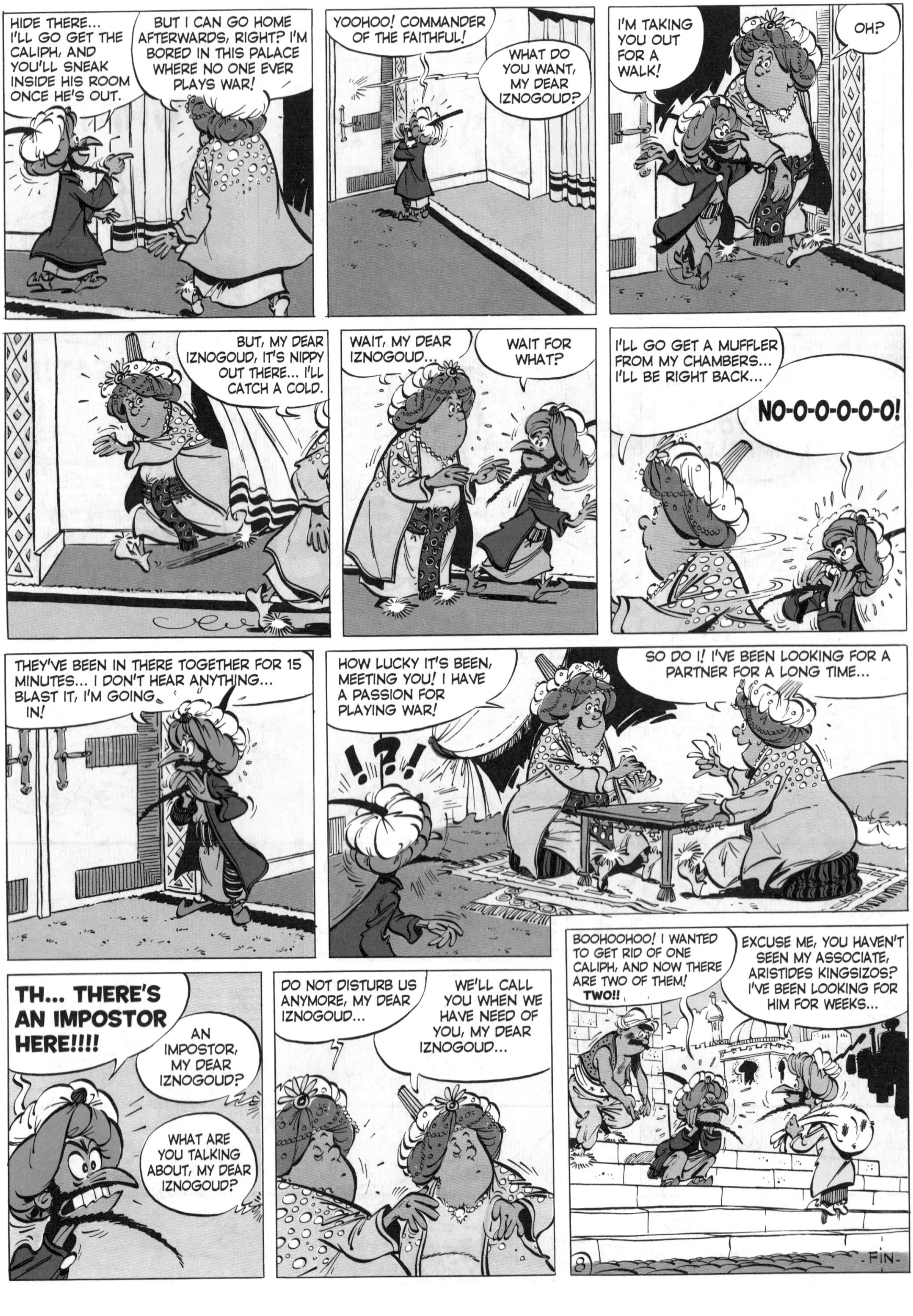
HIDE THERE... I'LL GO GET THE CALIPH, AND YOU'LL SNEAK INSIDE HIS ROOM ONCE HE'S OUT.
BUT I CAN GO HOME AFTERWARDS, RIGHT? I'M BORED IN THIS PALACE WHERE NO ONE EVER PLAYS WAR!
YOOHOO! COMMANDER OF THE FAITHFUL!
WHAT DO YOU WANT, MY DEAR IZNOGOUD?
I'M TAKING YOU OUT FOR A WALK!
OH?
BUT, MY DEAR IZNOGOUD, IT'S NIPPY OUT THERE... I'LL CATCH A COLD.
WAIT, MY DEAR IZNOGOUD...
WAIT FOR WHAT?
I'LL GO GET A MUFFLER FROM MY CHAMBERS... I'LL BE RIGHT BACK...
NO-O-O-O-O-O!
THEY'VE BEEN IN THERE TOGETHER FOR 15 MINUTES... I DON'T HEAR ANYTHING... BLAST IT, I'M GOING IN!
HOW LUCKY IT'S BEEN, MEETING YOU! I HAVE A PASSION FOR PLAYING WAR!
SO DO I! I'VE BEEN LOOKING FOR A PARTNER FOR A LONG TIME...
!?!
TH... THERE'S AN IMPOSTOR HERE!!!!
AN IMPOSTOR, MY DEAR IZNOGOUD?
WHAT ARE YOU TALKING ABOUT, MY DEAR IZNOGOUD?
DO NOT DISTURB US ANYMORE, MY DEAR IZNOGOUD...
WE'LL CALL YOU WHEN WE HAVE NEED OF YOU, MY DEAR IZNOGOUD...
BOOHOOHOO! I WANTED TO GET RID OF ONE CALIPH, AND NOW THERE ARE TWO OF THEM! TWO!!
EXCUSE ME, YOU HAVEN'T SEEN MY ASSOCIATE, ARISTIDES KINGSIZOS? I'VE BEEN LOOKING FOR HIM FOR WEEKS...
8
-FIN-

THE GIANTS' ISLAND

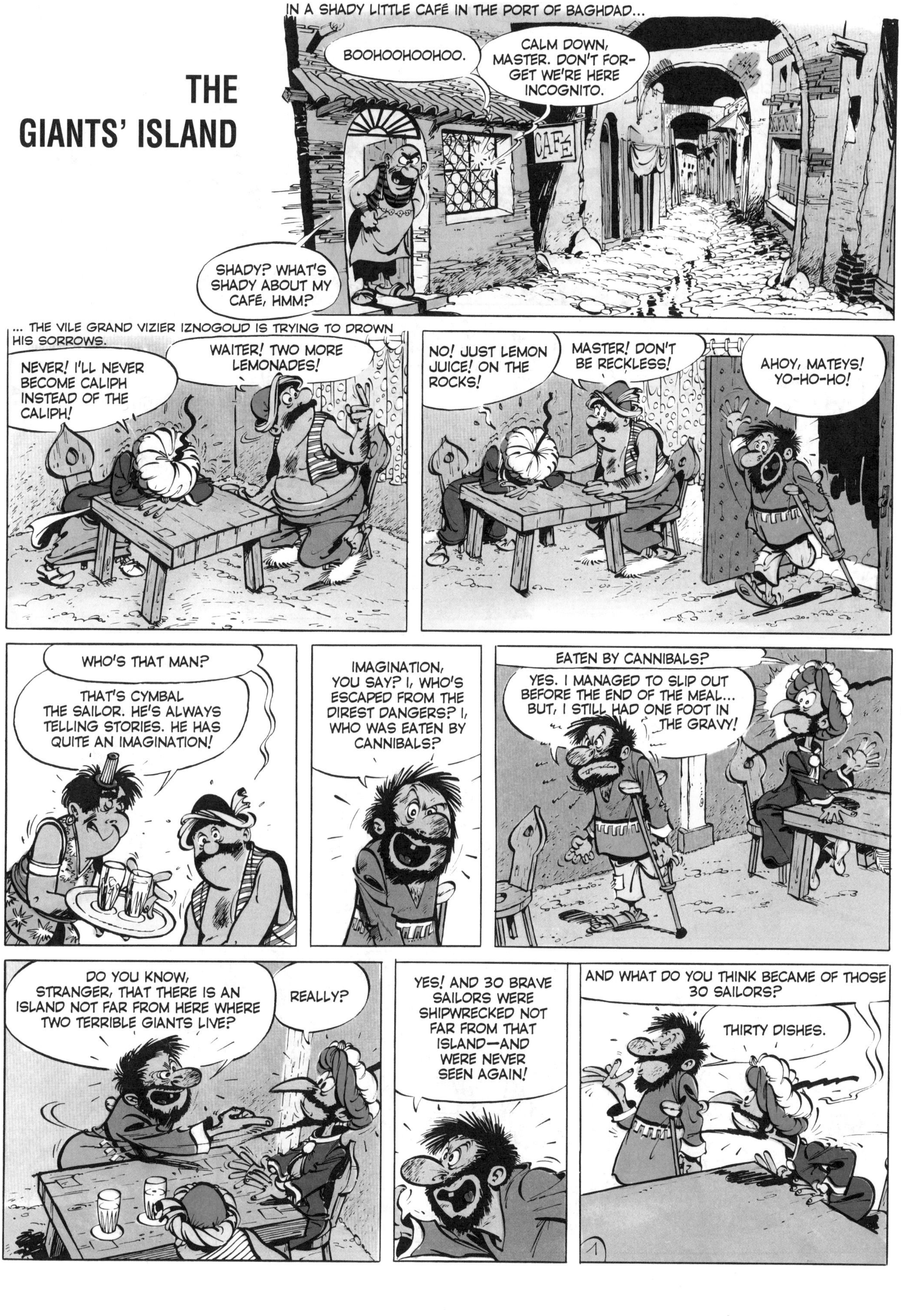
IN A SHADY LITTLE CAFÉ IN THE PORT OF BAGHDAD...
BOOHOOHOOHOO.
CALM DOWN, MASTER. DON'T FORGET WE'RE HERE INCOGNITO.
CAFÉ
SHADY? WHAT'S SHADY ABOUT MY CAFÉ, HMM?
... THE VILE GRAND VIZIER IZNOGOUD IS TRYING TO DROWN HIS SORROWS.
NEVER! I'LL NEVER BECOME CALIPH INSTEAD OF THE CALIPH!
WAITER! TWO MORE LEMONADES!
NO! JUST LEMON JUICE! ON THE ROCKS!
MASTER! DON'T BE RECKLESS!
AHOY, MATEYS! YO-HO-HO!
WHO'S THAT MAN?
THAT'S CYMBAL THE SAILOR. HE'S ALWAYS TELLING STORIES. HE HAS QUITE AN IMAGINATION!
IMAGINATION, YOU SAY? I, WHO'S ESCAPED FROM THE DIREST DANGERS? I, WHO WAS EATEN BY CANNIBALS?
EATEN BY CANNIBALS?
YES. I MANAGED TO SLIP OUT BEFORE THE END OF THE MEAL... BUT, I STILL HAD ONE FOOT IN THE GRAVY!
DO YOU KNOW, STRANGER, THAT THERE IS AN ISLAND NOT FAR FROM HERE WHERE TWO TERRIBLE GIANTS LIVE?
REALLY?
YES! AND 30 BRAVE SAILORS WERE SHIPWRECKED NOT FAR FROM THAT ISLAND—AND WERE NEVER SEEN AGAIN!
AND WHAT DO YOU THINK BECAME OF THOSE 30 SAILORS?
THIRTY DISHES.

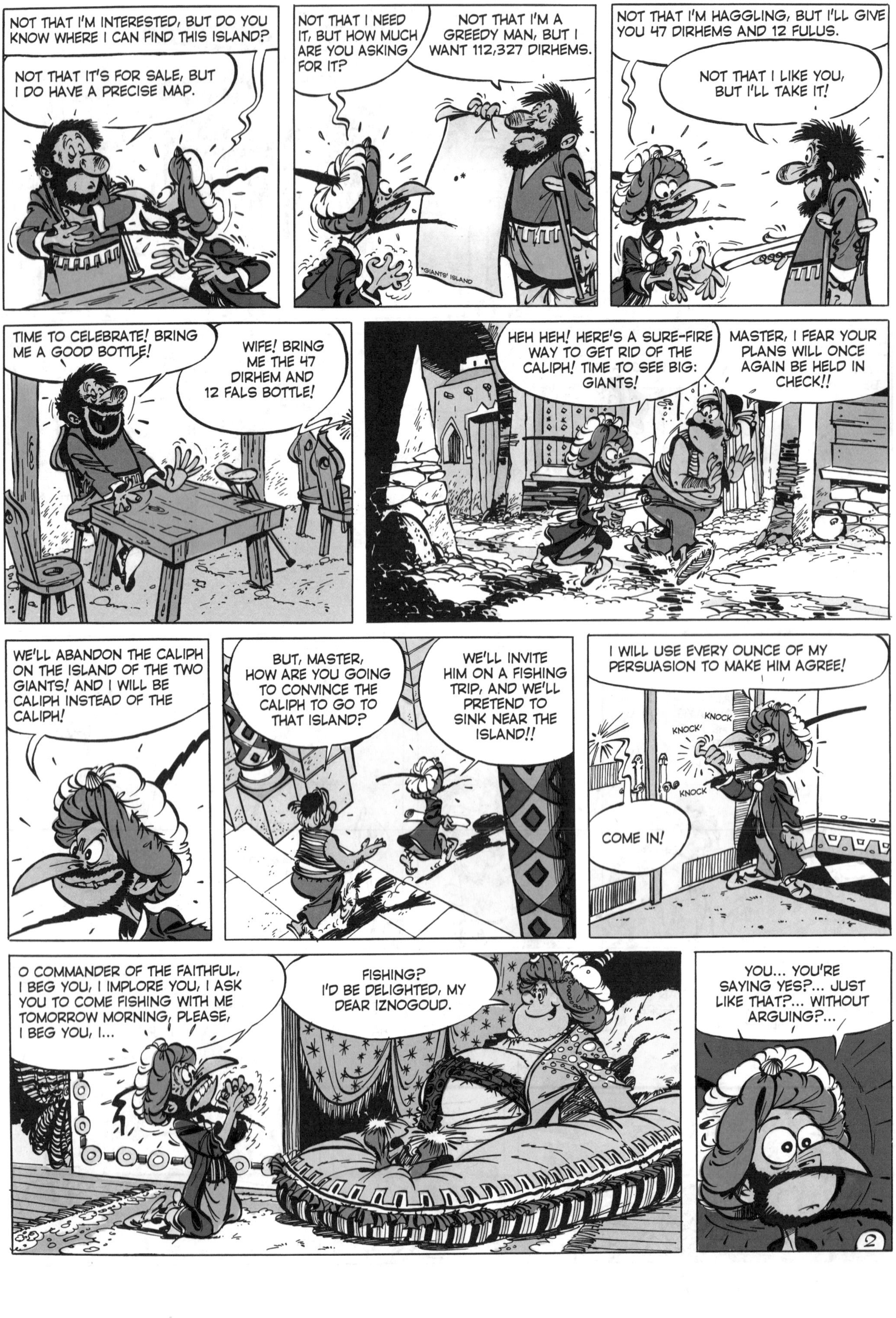

NOT THAT I'M INTERESTED, BUT DO YOU KNOW WHERE I CAN FIND THIS ISLAND?
NOT THAT IT'S FOR SALE, BUT I DO HAVE A PRECISE MAP.
NOT THAT I NEED IT, BUT HOW MUCH ARE YOU ASKING FOR IT?
NOT THAT I'M A GREEDY MAN, BUT I WANT 112,327 DIRHEMS.
*GIANTS' ISLAND
NOT THAT I'M HAGGLING, BUT I'LL GIVE YOU 47 DIRHEMS AND 12 FULUS.
NOT THAT I LIKE YOU, BUT I'LL TAKE IT!
TIME TO CELEBRATE! BRING ME A GOOD BOTTLE!
WIFE! BRING ME THE 47 DIRHEM AND 12 FALS BOTTLE!
HEH HEH! HERE'S A SURE-FIRE WAY TO GET RID OF THE CALIPH! TIME TO SEE BIG: GIANTS!
MASTER, I FEAR YOUR PLANS WILL ONCE AGAIN BE HELD IN CHECK!!
WE'LL ABANDON THE CALIPH ON THE ISLAND OF THE TWO GIANTS! AND I WILL BE CALIPH INSTEAD OF THE CALIPH!
BUT, MASTER, HOW ARE YOU GOING TO CONVINCE THE CALIPH TO GO TO THAT ISLAND?
WE'LL INVITE HIM ON A FISHING TRIP, AND WE'LL PRETEND TO SINK NEAR THE ISLAND!!
I WILL USE EVERY OUNCE OF MY PERSUASION TO MAKE HIM AGREE!
KNOCK
KNOCK
KNOCK
COME IN!
O COMMANDER OF THE FAITHFUL, I BEG YOU, I IMPLORE YOU, I ASK YOU TO COME FISHING WITH ME TOMORROW MORNING, PLEASE, I BEG YOU, I...
FISHING? I'D BE DELIGHTED, MY DEAR IZNOGOUD.
YOU... YOU'RE SAYING YES?... JUST LIKE THAT?... WITHOUT ARGUING?...
2

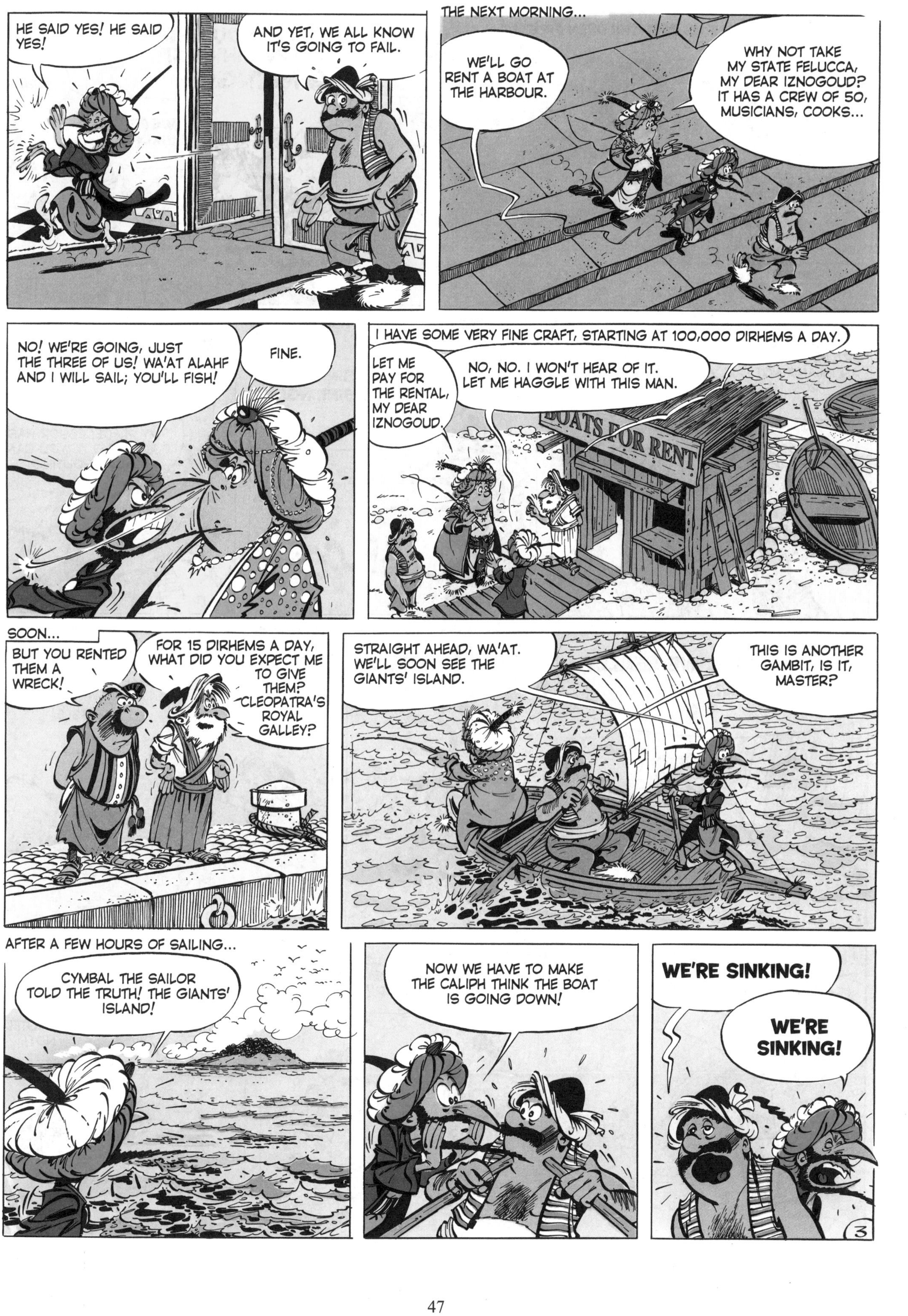
HE SAID YES! HE SAID YES!
AND YET, WE ALL KNOW IT'S GOING TO FAIL.
THE NEXT MORNING...
WE'LL GO RENT A BOAT AT THE HARBOUR.
WHY NOT TAKE MY STATE FELUCCA, MY DEAR IZNOGOUD? IT HAS A CREW OF 50, MUSICIANS, COOKS...
NO! WE'RE GOING, JUST THE THREE OF US! WA'AT ALAHF AND I WILL SAIL; YOU'LL FISH!
FINE.
I HAVE SOME VERY FINE CRAFT, STARTING AT 100,000 DIRHEMS A DAY.
LET ME PAY FOR THE RENTAL, MY DEAR IZNOGOUD.
NO, NO. I WON'T HEAR OF IT. LET ME HAGGLE WITH THIS MAN.
BOATS FOR RENT
SOON...
BUT YOU RENTED THEM A WRECK!
FOR 15 DIRHEMS A DAY, WHAT DID YOU EXPECT ME TO GIVE THEM? CLEOPATRA'S ROYAL GALLEY?
STRAIGHT AHEAD, WA'AT. WE'LL SOON SEE THE GIANTS' ISLAND.
THIS IS ANOTHER GAMBIT, IS IT, MASTER?
AFTER A FEW HOURS OF SAILING...
CYMBAL THE SAILOR TOLD THE TRUTH! THE GIANTS' ISLAND!
NOW WE HAVE TO MAKE THE CALIPH THINK THE BOAT IS GOING DOWN!
WE'RE SINKING!
WE'RE SINKING!
3

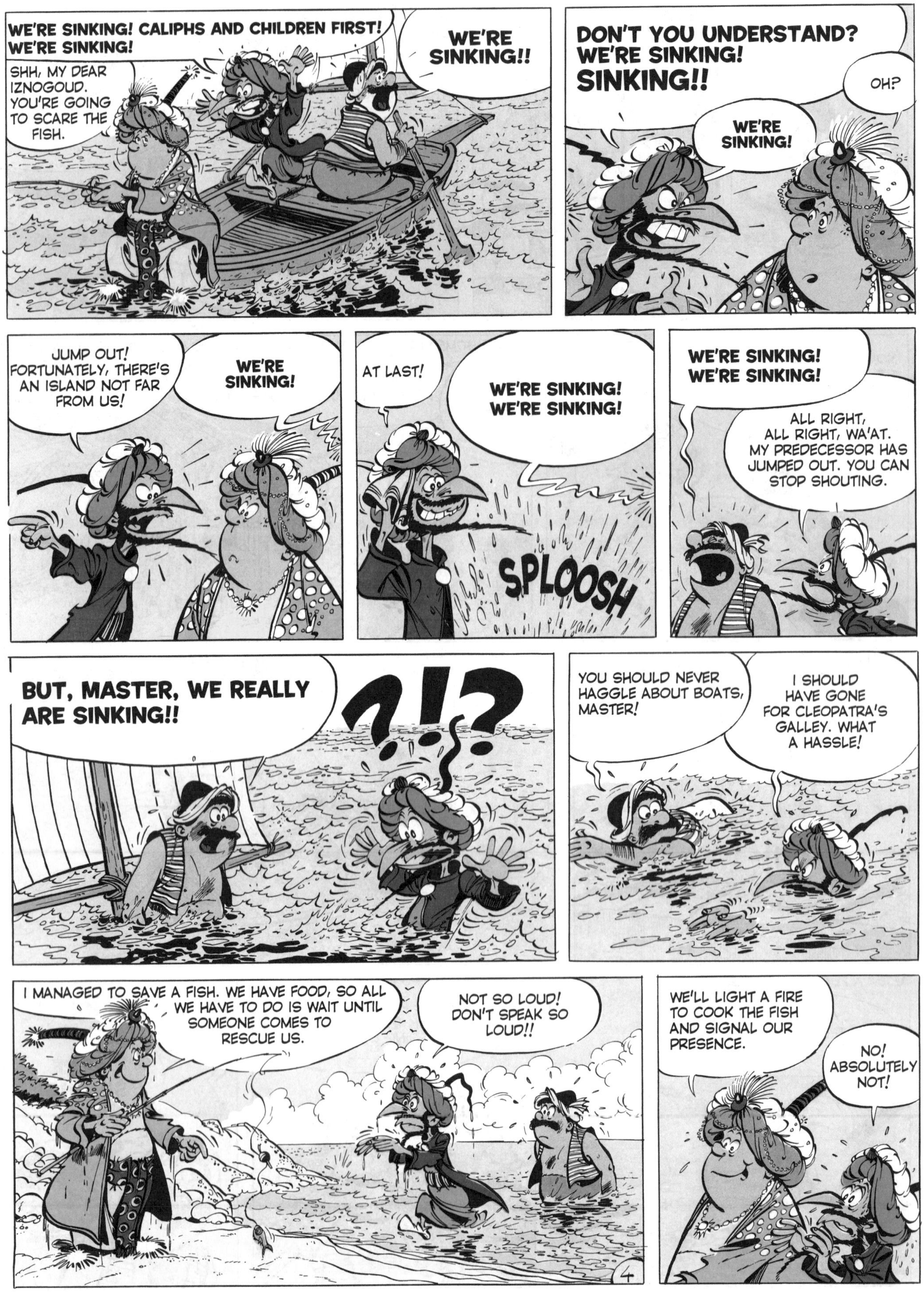

WE'RE SINKING! CALIPHS AND CHILDREN FIRST! WE'RE SINKING!
SHH, MY DEAR IZNOGOUD. YOU'RE GOING TO SCARE THE FISH.
WE'RE SINKING!!
DON'T YOU UNDERSTAND? WE'RE SINKING! SINKING!!
OH?
WE'RE SINKING!
JUMP OUT! FORTUNATELY, THERE'S AN ISLAND NOT FAR FROM US!
WE'RE SINKING!
AT LAST!
WE'RE SINKING! WE'RE SINKING!
SPLOOSH
WE'RE SINKING! WE'RE SINKING!
ALL RIGHT, ALL RIGHT, WA'AT. MY PREDECESSOR HAS JUMPED OUT. YOU CAN STOP SHOUTING.
BUT, MASTER, WE REALLY ARE SINKING!!
?!?
YOU SHOULD NEVER HAGGLE ABOUT BOATS, MASTER!
I SHOULD HAVE GONE FOR CLEOPATRA'S GALLEY. WHAT A HASSLE!
I MANAGED TO SAVE A FISH. WE HAVE FOOD, SO ALL WE HAVE TO DO IS WAIT UNTIL SOMEONE COMES TO RESCUE US.
NOT SO LOUD! DON'T SPEAK SO LOUD!!
4
WE'LL LIGHT A FIRE TO COOK THE FISH AND SIGNAL OUR PRESENCE.
NO! ABSOLUTELY NOT!

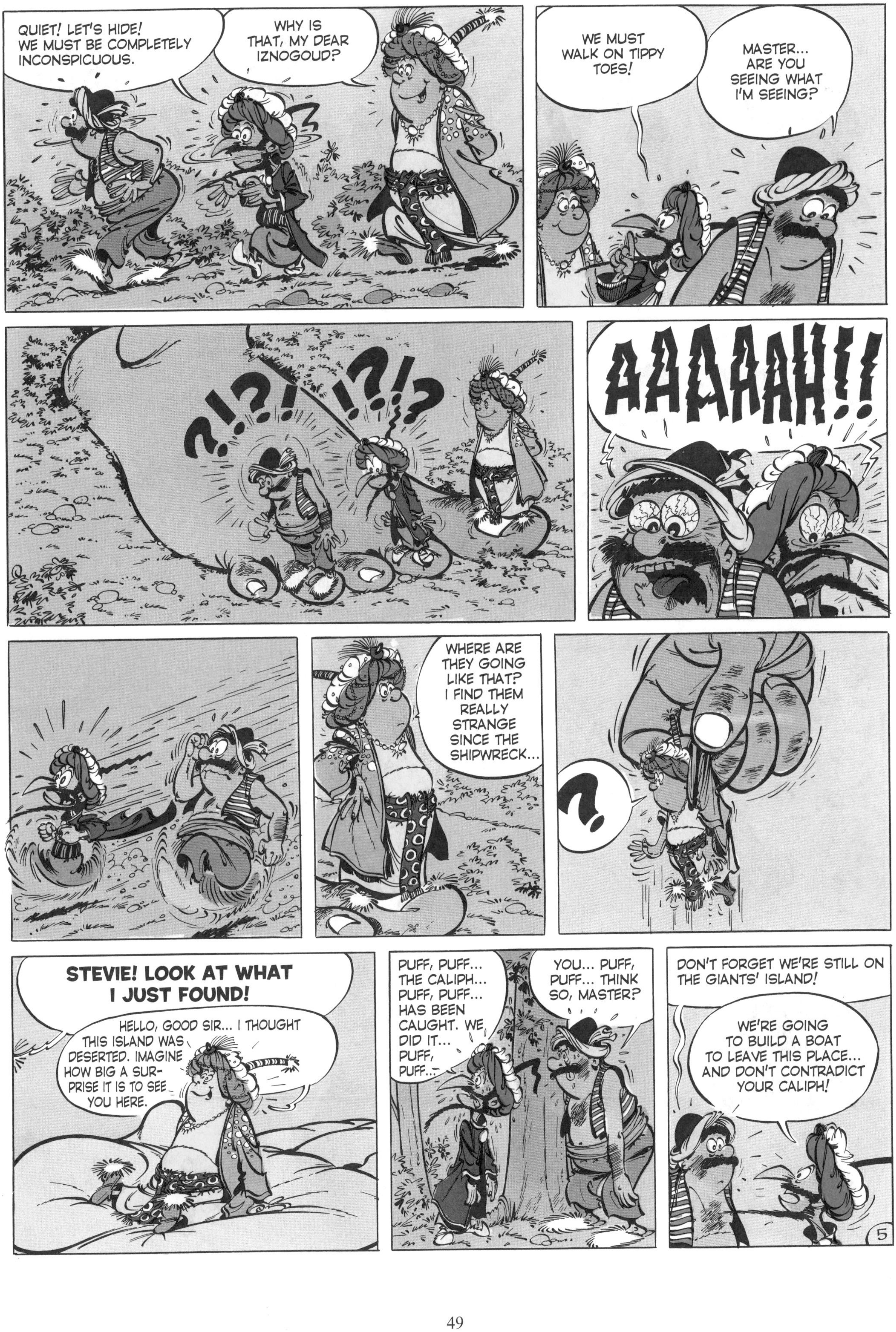
QUIET! LET'S HIDE! WE MUST BE COMPLETELY INCONSPICUOUS.
WHY IS THAT, MY DEAR IZNOGOUD?
WE MUST WALK ON TIPPY TOES!
MASTER... ARE YOU SEEING WHAT I'M SEEING?
?!?!
!?!?
AAAAAH!!
WHERE ARE THEY GOING LIKE THAT? I FIND THEM REALLY STRANGE SINCE THE SHIPWRECK...
?
STEVIE! LOOK AT WHAT I JUST FOUND!
HELLO, GOOD SIR... I THOUGHT THIS ISLAND WAS DESERTED. IMAGINE HOW BIG A SURPRISE IT IS TO SEE YOU HERE.
PUFF, PUFF... THE CALIPH... PUFF, PUFF... HAS BEEN CAUGHT. WE DID IT... PUFF, PUFF...
YOU... PUFF, PUFF... THINK SO, MASTER?
DON'T FORGET WE'RE STILL ON THE GIANTS' ISLAND!
WE'RE GOING TO BUILD A BOAT TO LEAVE THIS PLACE... AND DON'T CONTRADICT YOUR CALIPH!
5

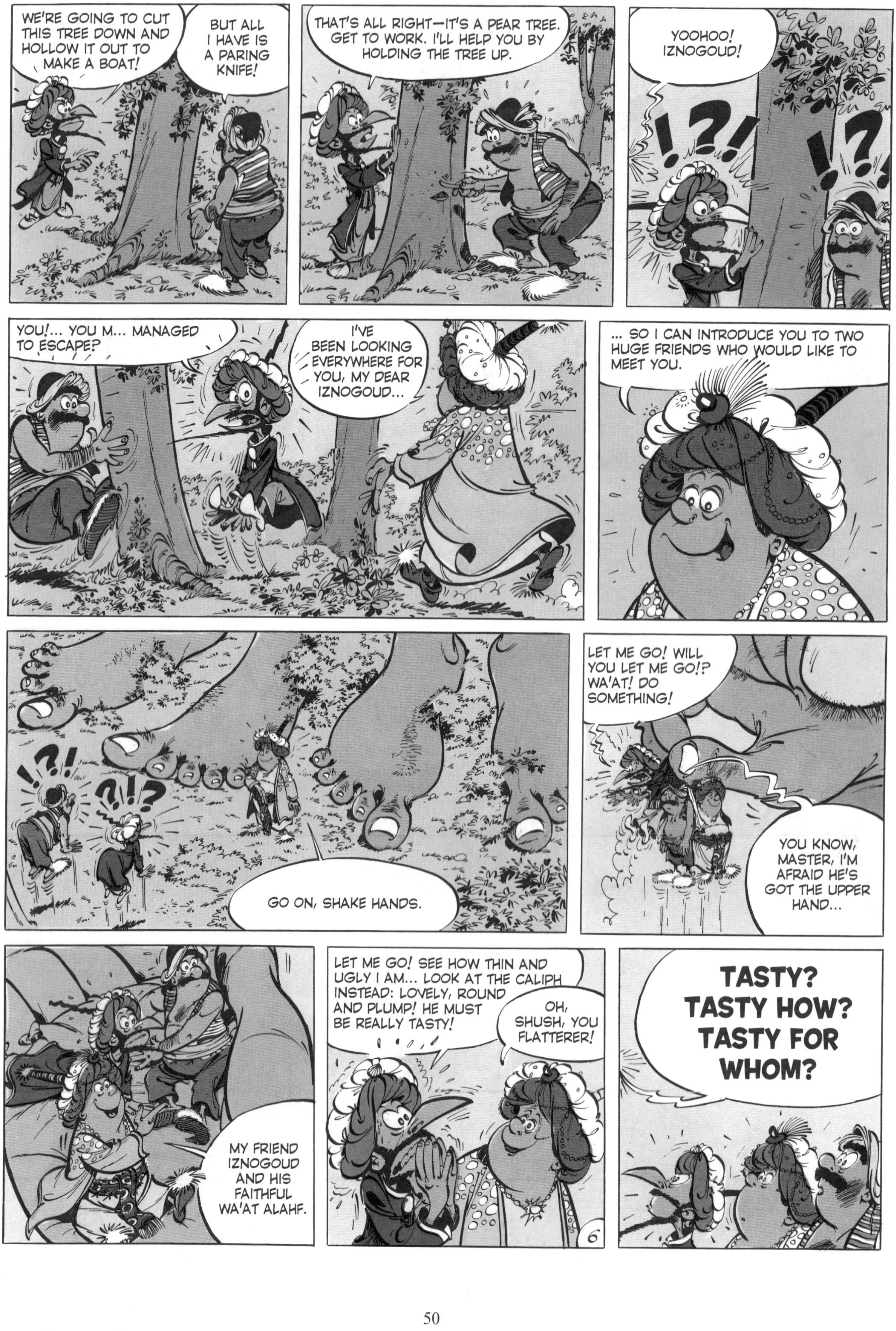
WE'RE GOING TO CUT THIS TREE DOWN AND HOLLOW IT OUT TO MAKE A BOAT!
BUT ALL I HAVE IS A PARING KNIFE!
THAT'S ALL RIGHT—IT'S A PEAR TREE. GET TO WORK. I'LL HELP YOU BY HOLDING THE TREE UP.
YOOHOO! IZNOGOUD!
!?!
!?!
YOU!... YOU M... MANAGED TO ESCAPE?
I'VE BEEN LOOKING EVERYWHERE FOR YOU, MY DEAR IZNOGOUD...
... SO I CAN INTRODUCE YOU TO TWO HUGE FRIENDS WHO WOULD LIKE TO MEET YOU.
!?!
?!?
GO ON, SHAKE HANDS.
LET ME GO! WILL YOU LET ME GO!? WA'AT! DO SOMETHING!
YOU KNOW, MASTER, I'M AFRAID HE'S GOT THE UPPER HAND...
MY FRIEND IZNOGOUD AND HIS FAITHFUL WA'AT ALAHF.
LET ME GO! SEE HOW THIN AND UGLY I AM... LOOK AT THE CALIPH INSTEAD: LOVELY, ROUND AND PLUMP! HE MUST BE REALLY TASTY!
OH, SHUSH, YOU FLATTERER!
6
TASTY? TASTY HOW? TASTY FOR WHOM?

HA, HA, HA! YOU HEAR THAT, STEVIE? HE THINKS WE'RE GOING TO EAT THEM!

WE'RE VEGETARIANS, STEVIE AND I... WE MOSTLY EAT VEGETABLE SOUP. IT'S GOOD FOR YOU—MAKES YOU GROW BIG AND STRONG!

BUT... THEN, WHAT DID YOU DO WITH THE 30 SAILORS WHO WERE SHIPWRECKED HERE?

HEY, THAT'S RIGHT, STEVIE! WITH THESE THREE, THAT'S 33. ONE TOO MANY!

SO, WHAT DO WE DO, STEVIE?

WE'LL DRAW LOTS TO CHOOSE WHICH ONES WE KEEP, LITTLE BUDDY!

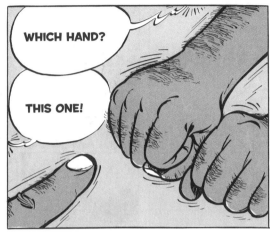

WHICH HAND?

THIS ONE!

ALL RIGHT, WE KEEP THIS ONE... YOUR TURN NOW!

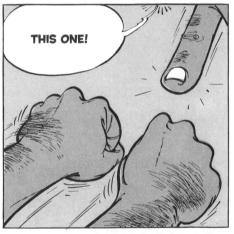

THIS ONE!

PITY, HE'S PRETTY UGLY... NEVER MIND, WE'LL KEEP HIM.

WHAT ABOUT ME?

WELL, WE'RE GOING TO SEND YOU HOME... STEVIE, BRING THE LITTLE TOY BOAT YOU PLAY WITH IN YOUR BATH!

THERE...

GET IN. WE'LL GIVE A GOOD PUFF AND SEND YOU HOME.

THANK YOU, GOOD SIRS.

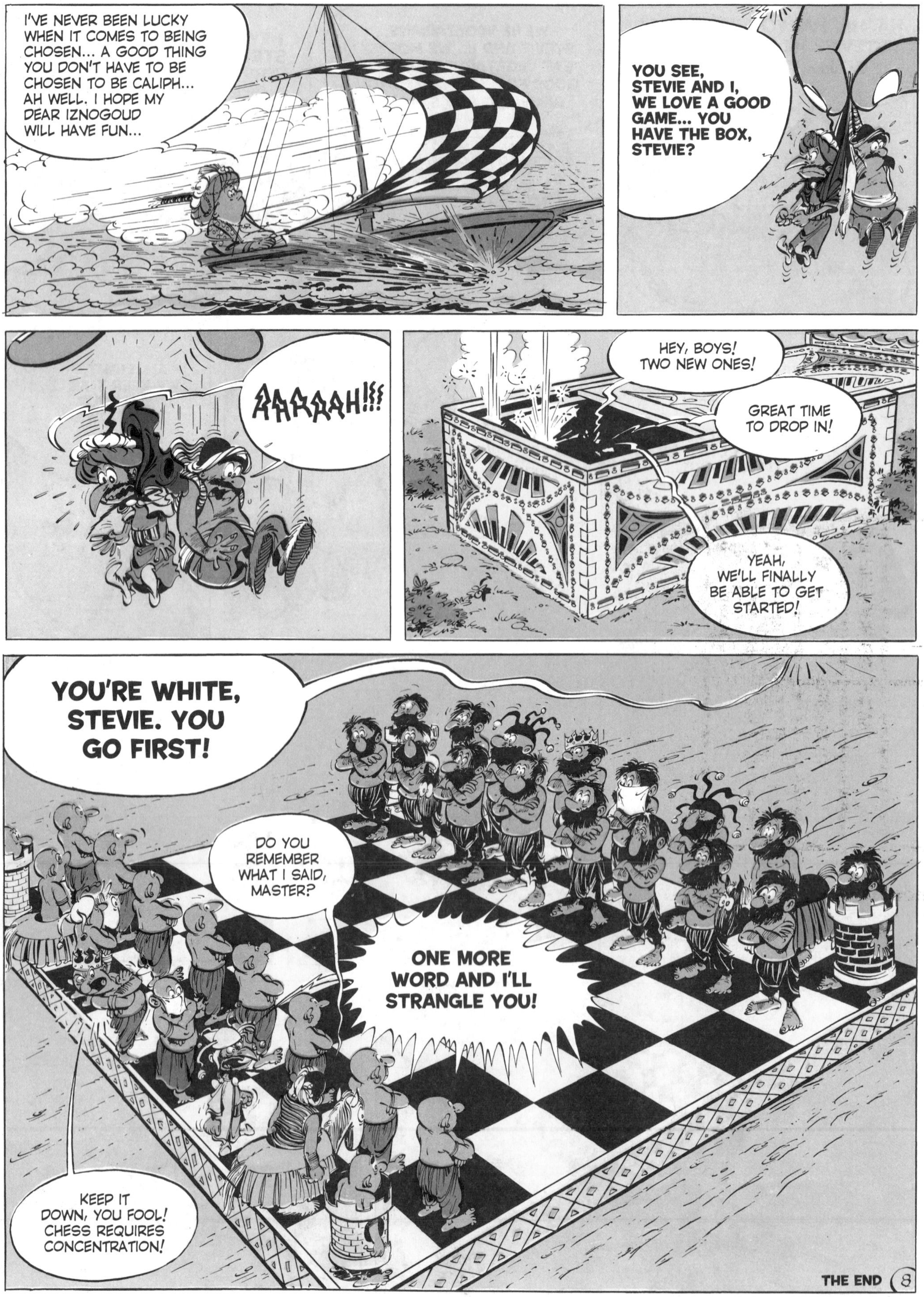
I'VE NEVER BEEN LUCKY WHEN IT COMES TO BEING CHOSEN... A GOOD THING YOU DON'T HAVE TO BE CHOSEN TO BE CALIPH... AH WELL. I HOPE MY DEAR IZNOGOUD WILL HAVE FUN...
YOU SEE, STEVIE AND I, WE LOVE A GOOD GAME... YOU HAVE THE BOX, STEVIE?
AAAAAAH!!!
HEY, BOYS! TWO NEW ONES!
GREAT TIME TO DROP IN!
YEAH, WE'LL FINALLY BE ABLE TO GET STARTED!
YOU'RE WHITE, STEVIE. YOU GO FIRST!
DO YOU REMEMBER WHAT I SAID, MASTER?
ONE MORE WORD AND I'LL STRANGLE YOU!
KEEP IT DOWN, YOU FOOL! CHESS REQUIRES CONCENTRATION!
THE END
8